ALSO BY KATE SEDLEY

The Plymouth Cloak

Coming soon from
HarperPaperbacks

Death and the Chapman

KATE SEDLEY

HarperPaperbacks

A Division of HarperCollins*Publishers*

This is a work of fiction. The characters, incidents, and dialogues are products of the author's imagination and are not to be construed as real. Any resemblance to actual events or persons, living or dead, is entirely coincidental.

HarperPaperbacks *A Division of* HarperCollins*Publishers*
10 East 53rd Street, New York, N.Y. 10022

A hardcover edition of this book was published in 1992 by St. Martin's Press.

Cover illustration by Michael Storrings

First HarperPaperbacks printing: April 1994

Printed in the United States of America

HarperPaperbacks and colophon are trademarks of HarperCollins*Publishers*

10 9 8 7 6 5 4 3 2 1

Death and the Chapman

PART I

May 1471
Bristol

CHAPTER

1

In this year of our Lord 1522 I am an old man. I've lived through the reigns of five kings; six, if you count young Edward. By my reckoning, I'm three score years and ten, the age, so the Bible tells us, which is man's allotted span on earth, and when my time comes, I shan't be sorry to go. Things aren't what they were, as I keep telling my children and grandchildren. And, come to think of it, as my mother told me.

"Things aren't what they were when I was a girl," she'd say, sweeping hard with her broom and sending the dust and bits of dead rushes flying out of doors, for all the world as though she were trying to sweep modern manners and modern thinking out with them.

I remember that little house in Wells as plainly as

though I'd been living there yesterday. My father, on the other hand, is a shadowy figure. Not surprising, really, because he died when I was barely four. He was a stone carver by trade, and very highly thought of, according to my mother. And it's true that when he died, following a fall from some scaffolding while working on the ceiling of the Cathedral nave, the Bishop—I forget his name, but he was the one before Robert Stillington—paid my mother a small pension out of his own pocket. I think, really, that's what started all her ideas, wanting me to have an education, to be able to read and write. Which is why she entered me as a novice with the Benedictines at Glastonbury.

Poor woman, she could never see that I wasn't cut out for the monastic life. I liked the outdoors. I liked being my own master. And I've absolutely no ear for music. My tuneless chanting at the daily offices would drive my fellow novices mad and was only one of the many reasons why they were glad to see the back of me. My good health, which I've kept all my life until recently, was another. The other monks and novices were constantly in and out of the Infirmary, especially in winter, but I don't recall ever having visited it once in all the time that I was at Glastonbury. And I've always had excellent teeth, never suffering much from toothache and its attendant ailments. One or two have gone now, of course, and a couple of others give me trouble when the wind's in the east, but what can you expect, at seventy?

But the real reason I left the Abbey and took to the road, after the death of my mother, was more fundamental than being resented by my fellow inmates. It was between me and God; and the Abbot, who was a wise and tolerant man, understood that. It's not that I doubt the existence of some other world, some hereafter. It's simply that I can never be quite certain that Christianity holds all the answers. Often walking through the oak and beech-woods, particularly at dusk, I've experienced something of the power which the ancient tree gods exercised over the minds of our Saxon ancestors. Those gnarled, arthritic branches, reaching towards me through the gloom, bring to life some race-memory. More often than I care to ad-mit, I've glanced fearfully over my shoulder, expecting, against all reason and faith, to see the figure of Robin Goodfellow or Hodekin or the terrible Green Man.

Mind you, this is a heresy I've kept to myself. I'm not such a fool as to say it out loud. And especially not now, when Pope Leo has just given King Henry the Eighth the title of *Fidei Defensor* for his written answer to the German monk, Martin Luther. And I'm only commit-ting pen to paper, because I feel I haven't all that much time left to me. Why do I feel like that? Nothing specific. Nothing I can put my finger on. Just a general feeling of malaise, a reluctance to get up in the mornings, a short-ness of temper with my daughter, my sons and their chil-dren. I'm tired of modern, forward-thrusting youth with their modern, forward-thrusting ways, and their unshak-able conviction that Henry Tudor and his son, our present King, rescued this country from the grip of a monster. It's my privilege to have met our late King Richard, even to have been of some use to him, God bless him!

But, nowadays, that's another heresy, and probably worse than the first one. The Richard people talk about now is a hunchbacked monstrosity, steeped in blood and evil. But that isn't the man that I remember, though I've no intention of writing a political tract: just a record of my early life, which in many respects was a strange one.

When my mother died, before I'd taken my final vows and I felt free to flout her wishes and leave the Abbey, I decided to become a chapman. An unlikely decision, you might think, for a lad who could read and write, hawking silks and laces and suchlike around the countryside. But after those years of being cooped up, hemmed in by rules and regulations, I needed the freedom. I needed to be my own master. I wanted to see different parts of this land of ours, which I knew only very slightly by reputation. Above all, I wanted to see London.

I find that strange now, back here in the heart of Somerset, looking out over the shadowed valleys and thickly-wooded hills, the scent of the warm-smelling earth strong in my nostrils. But in those days, London was my goal, the place where I was to make my fortune. I never did, of course. I wasn't cut out to be another John Pulteney or Richard Whittington. But if I didn't make much money, I did find that I had a talent in another direction. I found that I was good at solving puzzles, unraveling mysteries that baffled other people. And really, that's what these memoirs of mine are all about, in the hope that one day, when I'm dead, my children will be interested enough to read them.

It all began with the case of the disappearance of Clement Weaver, a young man I'd neither seen nor heard of that May morning in the year of Our Lord 1471. I hadn't long been on the road in those days. My mother had died the previous Christmas, and her thrift had meant that she was able to leave me a small—a very small—sum of money. With it, I had bought my first stock from an old peddler who was giving up the road to spend his dying years as a pensioner of the monks at Glastonbury, although I was unable to purchase his donkey. But I was young and strong, big and tall for my age, with broad shoulders, and quite capable of carrying my pack on my back. So I set off, full of confidence, walking up from Wells towards Bristol, stopping to sell my wares in the villages through which I passed. I spent May Day at Whitchurch, helping the villagers to bring in the may and then going to church to celebrate the feast of St. Philip and St. James; for me, a satisfying blend of the ancient tree-worship of our Saxon forebears and the demands of Holy Church which rule all our lives. I approached the walls of Bristol on May 2nd.

I could tell that something untoward was happening while I was still several hundred yards from the Redcliffe Gate. There was an unusual amount of activity, with armed men coming and going, and a crescendo of noise which permeated the town walls like water seeping through a dam. Near the church of St. Mary, tents and all the debris of men who had spent a couple of nights in the open indicated a military camp which was now being struck, the men scurrying about like ants, suggesting that they were in a hurry to be gone. Sudden orders to move on? I wondered. There was more than a hint of panic in the air.

As I neared the gatehouse, the town hermit, ragged, filthy and stinking to high heaven, scuttled out of his hovel to survey me, begging bowl hopefully extended.

One glance, however, at my youth, my patched and mended clothes, caused his weatherbeaten face to crumple with disappointment. He muttered something into his matted beard and disappeared again, quickly. Bristol was —still is—a very rich city, second in importance only to London, and he had no time to waste on the obviously poor and needy.

As I pushed my way into the gatehouse, the noise became deafening. It sounded as though an army were on the move. The watchman on duty was a surly, heavily pock-marked man whose naturally high complexion was now a fierce and dangerous red as he struggled to cope with, and control, the increased traffic of the archway. As well as the farmers and tradesmen going about their daily business, the roads were becoming increasingly choked with pilgrims on their way to Canterbury or Holywell or Walsingham, many of them stopping en route to see the sights of Bristol. And, added to this, soldiers continually tramped back and forth between the castle and the camp outside the city.

"What's happening?" I asked the watchman.

It was not the best moment I could have chosen. The man was in the middle of an acrimonious discussion with a big, raw-boned farmer concerning the amount of toll the latter had to pay on the sheep he was driving in to market. He paused just long enough to vent his spleen on me.

"Soldiers!" he spat. "That's what's bloody 'appening. Eating our victuals, drinking our wine and leaving us to pay the bleedin' bill!" And he turned back to the farmer, who had had time to get his second wind and was more convinced than ever that he was being overcharged.

I left them to it and stepped out into Redcliffe Street on the opposite side of the gate. By the time I reached the High Cross in the center of the town, progress was growing extremely difficult. The frequent paradings of foot-soldiers and the forays from the castle of mounted men-at-arms forced all other traffic almost to a standstill. And then, while I hesitated, wondering whether to start knocking on doors immediately or to find myself a meal at one of the inns—my big frame needed constant sustenance, another fact which had marked me out as unsuitable for monastic life—I suddenly found myself shoved unceremoniously to one side as a party of horsemen cleared a passage for two women riding in their midst. Along with the rest of the enforced spectators, I stared at them curiously. The older of the two looked neither to right nor left, imperiously oblivious of the tide of common life which surged around her. The thin, bitter face, seamed with wrinkles, showed the marks of suffering, and when a voice behind me muttered: "That's Queen Margaret," I realized with a shock that this must be Margaret of Anjou, the wife of King Henry the Sixth. But what was she doing here, in Bristol?

My gaze switched to her companion, a slender slip of a girl, who looked too fragile to control the big brown bay on which she was mounted. She wore unrelieved black and was obviously in mourning. A sudden breeze, whipping up High Street from the Backs, momentarily lifted the veil from her face to reveal a glimpse of deathly pallor and jutting bones, in which the eyes were just two dark smudges. Almost at once, she raised a gloved hand

and shrouded herself again in the clinging draperies. Then she was gone, along with the rest of the little cavalcade, clattering down Corn Street towards the bridge at the far end, which spanned the River Frome. We all stared after the dwindling figures for a moment, then stirred, grumbling about the delay before continuing with our business. Returning to the debate which had been my chief preoccupation before the interruption, I decided that the rumblings of my stomach merited my undivided attention, and asked the woman standing next to me for directions to any inn where they served a reasonable meal and did not give short measure on the ale.

She was a plump, homely body, not, I decided, quite as old as the network of fine wrinkles around the eyes at first indicated. The eyes themselves were dark brown, slightly opaque, conveying an impression of secrecy. But when she smiled, as she did after having carefully surveyed me from head to toe, they twinkled, giving her face an altogether pleasanter expression than it had worn hitherto. Her plain dress of homespun and home-dyed black broadcloth, and a complete absence of jewelry, indicated her lowly status and broke none of the sumptuary laws which Parliament so regularly pass and which we English as regularly ignore. The wisps of hair protruding from beneath her green woolen hood showed flecks of grey among the faded brown.

"Looking for somewhere to eat, are you?" she asked, sucking her lower lip and giving me the impression that she was playing for time while other thoughts took precedence in her mind. "Well, let me see . . . There's Abyngdon's, behind All Saints' Church, just down the road a bit, off Corn Street. Used to be called the Green

Lattis, but that's neither here nor there. Then there's the Full Moon, but that's usually crowded by midday with visitors to St. James's Priory. There's the White Hart at the end of Broad Street. Or the Running Man . . . On second thoughts, I wouldn't recommend that one. It was all right when Thomas Prynne was landlord—great friend he was, and still is, of my master—but he went to try his luck in London. Owns the Baptist's Head in Crooked Lane, off Thames Street . . ." Her voice tailed away and she stared into the distance, as though contemplating something there that she would rather not see. It was with a considerable effort that she pulled herself together and once more gave me her attention. "A peddler, are you?"

"Yes."

"Where have you come from? I'd say you're local, by the sound of you."

"I was born in Wells." I saw no need, at that point, to enlarge any further. "Thank you for your directions. I'll try Abyngdon's as it's nearest."

"Hold on." The woman laid a plump hand on my arm and I recall thinking that her grip was surprisingly tenacious. "It must be nearly midday. You're late for dinner. Ours was over nearly an hour ago. But if you like to accompany me while I run my errand, you can come home with me afterwards and I'll make sure you're fed. We keep a good table in Broad Street. Nothing's too good for an Alderman of Bristol."

I hesitated, suddenly unsure of my ground. She spoke with sufficient authority to make me wonder if perhaps I had been mistaken in assuming her lowly status.

"The Alderman is your husband?" I ventured.

She gave a deep-throated chuckle. "Get away with you! Do I look like the wife of an Alderman? No, of course not! He's my master. I keep house for him and his wife and . . . and his children." There was a slight hesitation, as though she were about to amend what she had said; then, evidently thinking better of it, she took my arm again, this time tucking one plump hand into the crook of my elbow. "If you'll give me your support as far as Marsh Street, we'll get on all the faster. I'm not as young as I was."

We set off along Corn Street, dodging the piles of filth in front of the houses and the mounds of offal outside a butcher's shop. There were plenty of pigs and goats, too, to impede our progress; they had no business, legally, to be kept within city limits; but the good citizens of Bristol ignored this regulation in the same way that people of other towns up and down the country ignored it. If there's one thing I've learned in my life, it's that the English see every law as a challenge, either to be circumvented or broken. I think the thing I remember most about that walk is the clamor of the bells. We'd heard them at Glastonbury, of course, sounding for the different offices of the day, but this was my first time in a city, and I'd never heard so many ringing all together; tolling the hours of the day, summoning citizens to meetings, warning of the opening of the municipal courts or simply calling the faithful to prayer at one of Bristol's many churches.

Marsh Street itself was full of sailors who had either just come ashore, intent on finding the nearest brothel, or were about to embark on one of the many ships at present riding at anchor along the Backs, laden with wine or soap or some other cargo destined for foreign shores. In front of one of the warehouses which lined the busy wharves was a carrier, loading his cart with bales of cloth which I learned later was woven by the weavers who lived and worked in the suburb of Redcliffe, on the opposite side of the Avon.

The carrier raised his head and, when he saw us approaching, lifted his hand in greeting.

"You're late, Marjorie," he said accusingly. "I'm almost ready to leave. What are my orders this time?"

"The same as usual. When you get to London, you're to go straight to the Steelyard. Deliver to the Hanse merchants and to nobody else." She turned to me, adding by way of explanation: "The Easterlings pay cash, which the Alderman insists on. Londoners want credit, he says, and then try to settle bad debts with all kinds of nonsense, such as tennis balls or packs of cards or bales of tassels." She chuckled again, drily. "They may get away with that in other parts of the country, but not in their dealings with Bristol." She put her hand into the pocket of her skirt and produced a piece of paper sealed with red wax, which she handed to the carrier. "And if you'd deliver this for me, I'd be obliged." A coin passed between them.

The man nodded cheerfully and tucked the letter inside his greasy, food-stained jacket. "Your cousin, is it? Never fear! I'll see it gets there. What about His High and Mightiness? Payment as usual, I suppose, *after* the job is done."

Marjorie smiled. "What else did you expect? You know the way the Alderman works as well as I do."

"It was worth asking, just in case, one day, a miracle

happens. I'll be off, then. Tell Alderman Weaver I'll see him in a week's time, when I get back." He nodded briefly at me and disappeared once more inside the warehouse. Further along the wharf, some sailors were acting the fool, lurching perilously close to the edge and singing a drunken shanty. *"Hail and howe, let the wind blow! The Prior of Prickingham has a big—"*

My companion gave an unconvincing shriek and clapped both hands over her ears.

"It's all right," I assured her gravely. *"Has a big toe* is what they're singing."

"I dare say. It's what they mean that matters." She added with mock severity: "The fools will be in the water in a moment and then they'll find themselves up before the Watch. However, that's their lookout, not ours. So, if you'll give me your arm again, we'll be off to Broad Street and that meal I promised you. By the way, what's your name?"

"Roger."

"And mine is Marjorie Dyer. That was my father's trade. He's dead now, God rest him!" She squeezed my arm and shuffled along beside me. "I'm sorry to be so slow, but this warm weather affects my legs. Cheer up! Not much farther to go now."

"Good," I said. "It's hours since my last meal. I'm starving."

CHAPTER
2

 I realize that, as yet, I've offered no explanation for the political events which were unfolding in Bristol on that warm May morning. Well . . . politics are boring. As are dates and facts. But in so far as those happenings and their sequel of some months later impinged, however slightly, upon my own story and the unraveling of my first mystery, I feel obliged to paint in the larger background. Briefly. I promise. And I can hardly expect the young tyros of the present generation, in their feverish preoccupation with New Worlds and New Learning, to try to unravel the tangled skein of events which was England in the last century. I knew precious little about it, myself, at their age. What I know now is the result of age, of reading, of piecing together fragments of conversation and knowledge gleaned over many years.

In the year 1399, King Richard the Second was deposed, and eventually murdered, by his cousin Henry of Bolingbroke, who usurped the crown as King Henry the Fourth.

The childless Richard's acknowledged heir was his cousin, Roger Mortimer, grandson of Edward the Third's third son, Lionel. Henry was the son of John of Gaunt, a younger son of that same monarch, and from this situation there arose, half a century later, a bloody dynastic struggle.

Richard Plantagenet, Duke of York, direct descendant of Roger Mortimer, claimed the crown from his cousin, King Henry the Sixth, Bolingbroke's grandson. York was driven to it by the unrelenting enmity of Henry's Queen, Margaret of Anjou, and was supported by his brother-in-law, the Earl of Salisbury, and Salisbury's eldest son, the Earl of Warwick.

The first blow was struck on May 22nd, 1455, and, five years later both York and Salisbury lost their lives at the battle of Wakefield. Six months after his father's death, York's eldest son was crowned King Edward the Fourth in Westminster Abbey.

At first, all went well, and this apparently easy-going young man of eighteen showed proper gratitude and respect for the architects of his victory, his mother's family of Neville, chief of whom was her nephew, the mighty Earl of Warwick.

In the year 1464, however, while Warwick worked tirelessly to bring about a French alliance through Edward's marriage to Bona of Savoy, Edward secretly married Elizabeth Woodville, the widow of the Lancastrian Lord Grey; a woman five years his senior and already the mother of two sons.

This marriage estranged not only the Earl of Warwick, but also Edward's brother, George, Duke of Clarence. The King's youngest brother, Richard, Duke of Gloucester, remained loyal, in spite of his hatred of the Woodville family.

Eventually, in 1469, the Nevilles kidnapped the King and attempted to rule the country through their prisoner. When this failed, Warwick tried to adduce Edward's bastardy and put the Duke of Clarence, who had married the Earl's elder daughter, Isabel, on the throne instead. When this plan also foundered, Warwick, Clarence and their wives, together with Warwick's younger daughter, Anne, fled to France. Here, the Earl, completely changing his tactics, made peace with the exiled Margaret of Anjou and agreed to restore the imprisoned Henry the Sixth to the throne. Anne Neville was married to Edward of Lancaster, Henry and Margaret's son.

In the autumn of 1470, the year before my story opened, three months before my mother died, eight months before I walked from Wells to Bristol, Warwick and Clarence returned to England with men and money supplied by King Louis of France. Partly through King Edward's own folly, he was out-generalled and caught in a trap. With the Duke of Gloucester and a handful of loyal friends, he fled to Burgundy, throwing himself on the mercy of Duke Charles, his sister Margaret's husband.

Elizabeth Woodville and her three little daughters, together with the Duke of Gloucester's two young children, sought sanctuary in Westminster Abbey, where the erstwhile Queen gave birth to a boy, named after his father.

Then, in March of the following year, Edward of York returned to reclaim his throne. Landing at Ravenspur, he and his youngest brother marched south almost without opposition. At Banbury, the Duke of Clarence joined them, deserting his father-in-law, and by early April Edward was in London.

Warwick, who had been in Coventry, suddenly moved against them, but on Easter Sunday was defeated and killed at Barnet. The next day, Margaret of Anjou, her son and daughter-in-law, landed at Weymouth to be met by the terrible news. Instead of attacking London, the Queen and her army marched north-west in an attempt to link up with King Henry's half-brother, Jasper Tudor, in Wales, entering Bristol at the end of April. A few days later she learned that King Edward was already at Malmesbury, racing across country to intercept her, and on May 2nd, that warm, sunny Thursday when I first heard the name of Clement Weaver, she and her troops left the city in a hurry; in a frantic bid to outpace King Edward.

We approached Alderman Weaver's house in Broad Street from the back and the narrow confines of Tower Lane. There was a little walled garden, as I remember, with a pear and apple tree, both thick with blossom, a bed of herbs and simples, a border of flowers along one wall and a lean-to privy. Marjorie Dyer produced a key from the heavy bunch attached to her belt and unlocked the door which led into the kitchen.

This was stone-flagged and strewn with rushes. An

iron pot suspended over the fire was obviously full of a stew intended for the family's supper. An iron frying-pan, a mortar-and-pestle, various ladles and spoons, basins and ewers were grouped together on the wooden table. Sides of salted beef and mutton hung from hooks in the ceiling. It reminded me of my mother's kitchen, except that it was much bigger. Well, let me be honest. We only had one living-room in my mother's house. I had never known the luxury of a parlor.

This house, which was several stories high, no doubt had a buttery and a hall as well as a parlor. And certainly more than one bedchamber. But there again, I knew nothing of bedchambers any more than I did of parlors. At home, I had slept on a truckle bed in one corner of the kitchen, and at the Abbey, in a dormitory with the other novices. This was the first gentleman's dwelling I had ever been in.

"Sit yourself down." Marjorie Dyer nodded towards a stool near the hearth, covered with a red and green cloth. "Leave your pack by the door and I'll look at it later. I'm short of needles and thread, if you have any."

I assured her that I had and thankfully slipped the heavy bundle from my back. I had been on my feet almost since sunrise and was beginning to feel tired. I slumped on to the stool she had indicated, keeping well away from the fire. Its heat was intense and the smoke was making my eyes water. As my companion bustled around, she appraised me with her shrewd brown eyes.

"You're a big lad. Nearly as tall as King Edward, I'd guess. And they say he stands over six feet."

"Have you ever seen him, then?" I asked, but with less curiosity than I might have displayed if the warmth hadn't begun to make me so drowsy. Marjorie handed me a mazer of ale, and the taste of the cold, bitter liquid went some way towards reviving me.

"A glimpse. Ten years ago when he visited Bristol. Very tall and very handsome, fair-haired, like you, and eyes the same shade of blue. The women all went wild about him." She grinned. "I reckon there were a few cuckolded husbands during that visit. They say he's a great womanizer."

Her tone of voice seemed to imply a question and I glanced up, shaking my head. "I'm still a virgin," I said. "There wasn't much chance to be anything else at the Abbey." I had given her a brief history of my life while we were walking from Marsh Street.

She gave a chuckle which slid into a full-throated laugh. "That's not what I've heard."

I shrugged. "Oh, I know there are stories about religious houses, and I've no doubt there's a certain amount of laxity in some of them. But we had a particularly strict Master of Novices."

It was her turn to shrug her plump shoulders. "You're young. There's no hurry." Her face shadowed again momentarily, as she cleared a space for me at the table. "Although, I shouldn't say that, I suppose. Youth alone is no guarantee of longevity." She motioned me to bring my stool over and went to spoon some of the stew on to a plate.

I got up and, carrying my now half-empty mazer in one hand and the stool in the other, I crossed the room and settled myself at the table. "I expect the plague will be rife again this summer."

Marjorie put the plate of steaming meat and vegetables in front of me. There was also some black bread, a piece of goat's milk cheese wrapped in a dock leaf, and a dish of those little green and white leeks which can be eaten raw. "I wasn't necessarily thinking of illness," she said. "There's . . . there's also accident . . . and . . . and murder." In the sudden silence which succeeded her words, all I could hear was the crackling of the fire.

I swallowed the spoonful of stew which I had shoveled into my mouth and repeated, "Murder?" It had not been just a casual remark, I could tell that by the way she spoke and looked. The word had a special significance for her.

She replenished my mazer from the vat of ale which stood near the door and drew up another stool to the table. "Forget I said anything. I shouldn't be discussing the family's troubles with a stranger."

I wiped my mouth on my sleeve. I was pretty uncouth in those days. "That's not fair," I protested. "You shouldn't arouse my curiosity and then refuse to tell me what it's about. Who do you know who's been murdered?"

Marjorie took one of the little leeks from the dish and began to nibble it. "It was just a remark. I didn't say I knew anyone." She glanced sideways at my skeptical expression and capitulated. "All right. Although I ought not to say anything, really. And besides, no one's sure that it is murder. At present, it's just a case of . . . disappearance."

"Whose disappearance?" I found myself intrigued, the more so now that my first pangs of hunger had been assuaged. In the distance, through the open kitchen door, came sounds of the bustling city, alive and vigorous in the warm spring weather.

"The Alderman's son," she said at last, reluctantly, as though wishing she hadn't spoken. Nevertheless, she went on: "He disappeared last winter in London."

I tore a piece off the loaf of bread. "You mean they never found a body? But in that case, what makes you think it's murder?"

"The circumstances of his disappearance." She leaned forward, folding her plump arms together on the table. "There was no reason for Clement to run away—if that's what you were thinking."

It was a possibility which had crossed my mind, I had to admit, and I wasn't going to abandon it in a hurry. "How old was Master Clement?"

"About as old as you. Maybe a little older."

I considered this information. "My mother always insisted that I was born in the same year as the Duke of Gloucester. So . . . I reckon I've seen nineteen summers."

My companion nodded. "That seems about right. Clement would have been about nine when King Edward visited Bristol."

"And ten years on, he's the age when he might well have quarreled with his father and decided to be his own master."

Marjorie shook her head. "No!" she said emphatically. "Clement got on well with his father, like his sister. The Alderman's an indulgent father. Over-indulgent, if you want my honest opinion. Ever since his wife died, a year ago last Michaelmas, Alison and her brother have meant everything to him. And now Alison's getting married he's going to be very lonely, but he won't do anything to stand in her way. There's no talk of postponing the marriage so he can keep her at home a bit longer. And I know plenty of men who would be selfish enough to do that, whatever you might be planning to say in defense of your sex."

"I'm not planning to say anything of the sort," I protested mildly. "I've no illusions about people's shortcomings, whether they're male or female. Humanity has a lot of failings."

"An old head on young shoulders," she mocked. "That I should live to see the day!"

I ignored this. "So Clement Weaver didn't disappear voluntarily. Didn't the Alderman make inquiries for him?"

"Of course he did, you stupid boy! He went to London himself, stayed there for months, with his brother and two of his nephews. They scoured the city from end to end. They even managed to enlist the help of Lord Stanley, but all to no avail. Clement was never found. He just disappeared from the face of the earth."

I had finished my stew by this time and looked significantly at my empty plate. Marjorie Dyer, somewhat to my surprise, took the hint and rose to fetch me a second helping. "You'll never want for asking," she commented drily.

Pointless to say that I hadn't uttered a word. Meekly, I accepted the refilled plate which she set before me, drained my mazer and attacked the food with relish. When I could speak once more, I said: "You've intrigued me. Having gone this far, why don't you tell me the whole story? That is, if you can spare the time. I can see you're a busy woman."

"Mmmm . . . And I can see you've a silver tongue when it suits you. A way of charming the birds off the trees, as my father would have said. And I shouldn't really spare the time to sit and chat with you. I've a junket to make for supper. However, there's not much to tell, and ten minutes or so won't make that much difference. Not if you're really interested, that is."

I nodded, unable to reply because my mouth was full. But before she could begin, there was an interruption. The door leading from the hall opened and a girl about my own age, or a little younger, came into the kitchen. This, I assumed, correctly as it happened, was the daughter of the house, Alison Weaver.

She wasn't a girl you could really call pretty; her nose was too large and the wide mouth a little too decided. But she had lovely eyes, a soft hazel, flecked with green and fringed with very long, very thick lashes. Her skin was honey-colored, and she had made no attempt to whiten it, as was fashionable. She was thin, with tiny hands and feet, but had a wiry kind of strength which, at second glance, detracted from my first impression of a soft and yielding vulnerability.

"Marjorie—" she began, then stopped abruptly. "Who's this?" she demanded, staring at me and my plateful of stew.

Marjorie, I thought, seemed a little flustered; a little nervous of a girl she must have known since childhood. It was almost as though there were some antipathy between them.

"He's a chapman. He gave me his arm as far as Marsh Street because my legs were bad." She was defensive, improvising, and sent me a quick, covert glance which told me plainly not to contradict her. And, indeed, it was the truth as far as it went. "I was feeling faint and he brought me home. I felt the least I could do was to offer him something to eat."

The girl continued to stare at me, then nodded briefly. "All right," she said. "As long as you don't make a habit of it. You know Father's rules about the servants entertaining strangers." I looked at Marjorie and saw the faint stain of red on her cheeks, the badge of her resentment, and wondered fleetingly why she stayed here. A number of reasons presented themselves, but before I could formulate them properly in my mind, Alison Weaver addressed me. "What sort of merchandise do you carry?"

I dropped the spoon on my plate and wiped my mouth hurriedly, this time on the back of my hand. "I . . . I have s-some very fine lace," I managed to stutter. "And some very pretty colored ribbons. Needles, threads, toys . . . The usual sort of things," I finished lamely.

I could see by her dark green gown of very fine wool, with its trimming of sable, that money was no object to the Alderman when it came to his daughter's clothing. A coral rosary was wrapped around her left wrist, and a black-enamel and gold cramp ring adorned one finger. She had other rings, some of them set with precious stones, and several gold chains around her neck. It was not difficult to see that her father was a man of substance. I doubted if she would be interested in the sort of things that were in my pack.

As I say, I was young then, and had been out of the world for a number of years. I didn't appreciate, as I do now, that women can never resist the prospect of buying, particularly if it's for the adornment of their bodies.

"Show me!" she commanded.

I rose hastily and fetched my pack from the corner, while Marjorie Dyer cleared more space on the table so that I could lay out my stock. I had been pleased with it when I bought it off the old peddler, but it looked little enough now that it was on display. Or perhaps it was simply that I was seeing it as I imagined Alison Weaver was seeing it, appraising it against the goods she could buy in the shops of Bristol and London. But I need not have worried. Without even glancing at anything else, she stretched one thin brown hand instinctively for the best thing there, a length of figured, ivory-colored ribbon. She held it up to the light, letting it cascade through her fingers in a shimmering waterfall to the dusty floor. For the first time since entering the kitchen, she smiled.

"It's beautiful. Look, Marjorie! I shall use it to trim the neck of my wedding gown. I'll take it. All of it." She did not even ask the price. "Pay the man, Marjorie. I've no money on me. Father will give it back to you when he comes home." Marjorie, none too pleased, as I could tell, shuffled away to get her purse while Alison waved me back to my seat at the table. "You might as well finish your meal."

I thanked her politely, repacked the rest of my stuff, told Marjorie the cost of the ribbon and pocketed the money before sitting down again to my stew, which had now gone cold and congealed on the plate. It looked grey and unappetizing and I no longer fancied it, so I pushed it to one side and finished my ale. I was just about to say I must be going, when Alison Weaver drew up another stool and sat down beside me.

"What were you both talking about," she demanded accusingly, "when I came in?"

CHAPTER
3

There was an uneasy silence, and I could see that Marjorie Dyer was debating with herself whether to tell the truth. I drained the dregs of my ale and read the little rhyme carved into the wooden base of the mazer. "*If you would a Goodman please, Let him rest and take his ease.*" A fine sentiment, no doubt, but not one many Goodwives were prepared to abide by. And, indeed, why should they? Most of them worked hard from sunrise to sundown. I know my mother did. I'm not talking about the nobility, you understand, or even Alderman Weaver's daughter. At this point in my life, I knew very little about such women.

Marjorie cleared her throat, but her mistress was quicker. "You were talking about Clement, weren't you?

You know Father doesn't like you discussing our business with strangers! You're a gossip, Marjorie, and you know what happens to gossips. They get ducked in the pond.'' The girl then seemed to relent, but I could see by the expression on Marjorie's face how deeply she resented the reprimand, particularly in front of me. Once again, I wondered what the real relationship was between her and the family. She seemed, on one hand, to hold the privileged position of an old and trusted retainer, but on the other to be everybody's whipping-boy. Alison Weaver went on: "Oh well, I suppose there's no harm done. How much have you told him?''

"Only that Master Clement disappeared last winter in London.''

"And hasn't been heard of since," I added. "Other than that, I know nothing, so you need have no fear that I shall be bruiting your family business abroad. I'll be on my way.''

I half rose from my stool, but the girl waved me down again. She had an air about her of one accustomed to being obeyed, and in those days I was unused to standing up for myself. She looked at me with curiosity.

"You don't talk like any chapman I've ever met. Who are you?" So I recounted my life's history once more and was gratified to note that by the end of it she was regarding me for the first time as though I were a human being and not a part of the furniture. I could tell, too, that she liked what she saw. I was a good-looking youth at that age, even if I do say so myself. When I'd finished speaking, she rested her elbows on the table and propped her chin between her hands; little hands that gave small, fluttering movements like captive birds.

"Would you care to hear the whole story," she asked me, "about my brother's disappearance?"

"If you would care to tell it me," I answered gravely.

"What do you think, Marjorie? Would Father mind?"

Marjorie shrugged her plump shoulders. "He might, but he's not here, is he? And won't be for an hour or two yet. He's gone to a Guild meeting, and afterwards to a service at the Temple Chapel." She added for my benefit: "It's the Weavers' chapel, dedicated to St. Katherine, their patron saint."

Alison copied the housekeeper's shrug. "In that case, what he doesn't know won't hurt him."

I have never ceased to marvel, all my life, at the pragmatism of women: I think they are born without scruples. Nevertheless, I have been thankful for it on many occasions, as I was thankful for it then, because my curiosity had been aroused, and to leave with it unsatisfied would have been like denying a man dying of thirst a drink. And as though she read something of my thoughts, Marjorie Dyer asked: "Shall I pour us all some ale?"

Her mistress nodded. "And open the door a little more. It's close in here with the heat of the fire."

The housekeeper took my empty mazer and reached two more down from a shelf, filling all three from the cask of ale. Then she stood the door wide, letting in the fragrant scents of the garden. The afternoon had turned extremely warm and there was a faint shimmer of heat in the air. The light quivered as bright as a sheet of pressed metal, and the faint, far cry of a bird was, for a moment, the only sound on the still, spring air. Then the noises of the city seeped back, like a slowly rising tide.

Alison Weaver sipped her ale and fingered the coral rosary around her wrist. "I don't know where to begin," she said.

"Begin with your journey to London. There's nothing much to tell before that."

Marjorie, I thought, spoke with unnecessary sharpness, but looking at her, I could see that she was upset. Clement Weaver had probably been her favorite; less imperious, perhaps, than his acid-tongued sister. I had a mental picture of a sweet, soft-spoken boy, deeply affected by his mother's death.

Alison nodded, sipped more ale, then resumed her former position, elbows on the table, chin propped between her hands. "It was before Christmas, last year," she began, "around All Hallowstide . . ."

She had recently become betrothed to William Burnett, the son of another of Bristol's Aldermen and a fellow member of the Weavers' Guild. The Burnetts, I gathered, were even more well-to-do than the Weavers themselves, owning up to a hundred looms in the suburb of Redcliffe and claiming kinship with a nobleman who lived in the village of Burnett, some miles outside the city. It was an alliance, therefore, to gratify the one family more than the other, and Alderman Weaver was determined that no expense should be spared on arrangements for the wedding. In particular, his daughter's brideclothes should be the best that money could buy and Bristol merchants were deemed unworthy of providing the necessary materials. Alison was despatched to London, in the company of Clement, to stay with her uncle and aunt, the Alderman's brother and his wife. John Weaver, also employed in the cloth trade, had elected many years previously, on the occasion of his marriage, to try his fortune in the capital and was now, it seemed, nearly as rich—although, gratifyingly, not quite as rich—as his elder brother. He and his wife lived in the ward of Farringdon Without, which, so Alison informed me, taking pity of my self-confessed ignorance of London and its byways, included Smithfield cattlemarket, the Priory of St. Bartholomew and the Temple and its gardens, which ran down to the River Fleet. It was, moreover, within easy reach of the Portsoken ward, where the weavers had their dwellings.

"You were both to stay with your uncle and aunt?" I queried, when Alison paused for a moment. "Both you and your brother?"

But this, apparently, was not the case. John Weaver and his wife, Dame Alice, had two grown sons, one of whom was married and had not yet left home to set up on his own. Although a truckle bed could therefore be offered to Alison, there was no room for Clement. He was to lodge, as the Alderman himself did when in the capital, at the sign of the Baptist's Head in Crooked Lane, off Thames Street; an inn owned and run by his old friend from Bristol, Thomas Prynne.

"You remember, I told you," Marjorie said with a nudge, "he was landlord of the Running Man before he decided to try his luck in London."

I recollected and nodded. "You were reluctant to recommend the inn now that Thomas Prynne is no longer there."

"A good man," Marjorie confirmed. "Greatly liked and very much missed in Bristol. He and the Alderman were close friends. They grew up together in Bedminster village.''

Alderman Weaver had plainly outstripped his boyhood companion and, by the same token, was a self-made man, not the heir of inherited wealth as his children were. Children? Or child? I glanced again at Alison, which prompted her to continue.

"As I was saying—'' here she darted a look at the housekeeper as though resentful of being interrupted— ''Clement was to stay at the Baptist's Head." She conceded: ''Marjorie's right about Thomas Prynne. My father has known him all his life. When we were little, Clement and I used to call him Uncle Thomas, although my mother objected. She was a de Courcy, you see.'' She spoke as if this explained everything, as in some ways it did. The name indicated descent from the old Norman aristocracy, and the Alderman, on his way up, had no doubt considered such a marriage advantageous. I wondered idly how much dowry the lady had brought him. I suspected little. My guess was an impoverished family with pretensions, but fallen on hard times, forced to ally itself with ''new'' money. I speculated on the probable happiness of such a union. Alison continued, recapturing my wandering attention: ''Father would never let Clement stay anywhere else in London. And especially not on that occasion. It was absolutely necessary that my brother should lodge with someone he could trust.''

I took another gulp of ale. ''Why?'' I asked, although I could already guess the answer.

Alison Weaver twisted the black and gold cramp ring on her finger. ''He was carrying a great deal of money on him, money for me to buy my bride-clothes with.''

"How much?" I asked, forgetting in my eagerness for details that I was a lowly chapman and she the daughter of an Alderman. I felt Marjorie kick me under the table.

Alison, however, was too wrapped up in her story to notice my impertinence, or to make anything of it if she did. She must, during the past months, have gone over and over the events in her mind.

"A hundred pounds," she said in an awed voice. "One hundred and fifty marks. Some of it, mind you, was for payment to the Easterlings at the Steelyard. My father told me afterwards that he had unintentionally overcharged them for a consignment of cloth and had instructed Clement to reimburse them while he was in London."

"A great sum of money for a young man to be carrying." Marjorie interrupted. "It was asking for trouble if you want my opinion."

"Nobody does!" her mistress replied tartly. "And in any case, no one knew how much he was carrying, not even me. There was no reason for anyone to suspect that he had such an amount about his person."

"Footpads and thieves," I pointed out gently, "take their chances. Anything and everything is grist to their mill. Two marks are as much worth stealing as twenty. And if the haul turns out to be a large one, that's simply their good fortune."

"Precisely what I said!" Marjorie nodded sagely. "I only wish I'd known how much money the Alderman had entrusted to Master Clement. I should have tried to talk him out of it, or persuaded him to go himself. A young man on his own, carrying a purseful of gold, is asking for trouble! And in an evil city like London!"

Alison jumped to her feet, the hazel eyes blazing. The green flecks seemed to disappear, swamped by her anger.

"Shut up, Marjorie! Shut up! It's easy enough to be wise after the event."

I felt this to be a little unfair. Marjorie, had she been in possession of all the facts, would, according to her own account, have been wise before the event, and whatever had happened to Clement Weaver might have been prevented. I agreed silently with her that the Alderman had been foolish, and in consequence felt obliged to take her part.

"I have heard," I offered tentatively, "that London is a very dangerous place." I noticed that since we had begun talking, the light had changed. Through the open kitchen door, the trees and distant rooftops, visible above the garden wall, were painted with sudden sharp brilliance against a sky which had faded from blue to pearl-grey. The day, which had been so fine, would end in rain, and as though to confirm this impression, from far off came a faint rumble of thunder. I made to rise again. "I should be on my way. I have my living to make and lodgings to find before the storm breaks."

Alison turned her small, neat head in my direction. "Sit down," she ordered. "You haven't heard the end of the story." She added on a suddenly fretful note: "Don't you want to?"

"Very much." And that was the truth. "It's just that I've sold nothing today beyond the ribbon you bought off me. I need money if I'm to sleep dry and safe tonight and not under a hedge."

She resumed her seat at the table, willing me to do the same. Against my better judgment, I complied. "You can sleep here tonight," she said, astonishing both Marjorie and myself, "by the kitchen fire. I'll speak to Father about it when he comes home."

I realized afterwards, looking back, that her brother's disappearance must have occupied most of her waking thoughts and possibly many of her dreams as well. It had no doubt been the main topic of conversation between herself and all those close to her for the last five months. They had talked around it in circles until they had nothing new to say on the matter. Each one proffered the same jaded point of view. She needed a fresh mind, fresh thoughts, before she could finally accept that there was no solution to the puzzle; that her brother was gone and would probably never be seen alive again. Because I have to admit, from what I had already heard, that that was the most likely outcome. A wealthy young man, set upon and murdered for his money, his body disposed of in the nearest river, was that so unprecedented? It was one of the hazards of everyday life. And didn't the Scriptures tell us that man born of woman had but a short time to live? Murder, rapine, famine, plague, they were all God's instruments.

With a start, I realized that I was thinking as I had been taught to think, expected to think, by the monks who had been my teachers. It was partly to escape their abject acceptance of the inevitability of Divine Will that I had decided against taking my final vows.

"Your father will never permit of his sleeping here,"

Marjorie protested. "The chapman should be gone before the Alderman returns."

"I've told you, I'll speak to Father." Alison dismissed the housekeeper's objections and turned to me. "Well? Will you stay? The price I paid for that ribbon is sufficient, I should have thought, to let you eat for at least a couple of days."

"That I paid," Marjorie muttered under her breath, but not so low that her words were unaudible. I expected her mistress to fly into another fit of passion, but Alison ignored her, raising her eyebrows once again at me.

"If you're certain that your father won't mind, I should be grateful for the chance of a warm fire and decent food." The first drops of rain had started to fall and I could hear their faint pattering on the leaves of the trees. The air was heavy and windless, but the tiniest of soughing noises among the branches indicated a rising breeze. It could be a cold wet night.

"Leave Father to me." Alison spoke with authority. "Now, what point had we reached in the story?" And without waiting for, or needing, a reply from either of us, she continued: "The circumstances were not what you think. Nor what Marjorie has led you to believe. My brother was not roaming the streets of London with such an amount of money in his pocket. We left Bristol on All Hallows' Day, and two of our men, Ned Stoner and Rob Short, went with us. My maid Joan rode pillion behind Ned. We spent three nights on the road and my father hired four other men to go with us as far as Chippenham. When we neared London, my uncle sent two of his servants as far as Paddington village to accompany us into the city and guide us to our destinations." She paused for breath, and once more there came the distant rumble of thunder, but closer this time. The noise of the rain increased.

"You were well protected, then," I said.

She nodded. "For most of the time. And even when there were only the five of us, we travelled with a party of merchants whom we had met at one of the inns where we stayed. My father had advised us to do that, and we obeyed him."

"So?" I prompted, when she seemed to have fallen into a reverie. "What happened when you finally reached London?"

"What? Oh! It was raining hard and had been for the most of the day, so my uncle and aunt had sent their coach for me and my maid. But Clement's mare, Bess, had cast a shoe and it was agreed, in order to save time— it was late afternoon by now and beginning to get dark, you see—that he should ride in the coach with us, and that Ned would return to Paddington the following morning to collect Bess from the smithy. We therefore went first to the Dowgate Ward to let my brother alight, before continuing to Farringdon. He got out at the corner of Thames Street and Crooked Lane."

"Alone? Why didn't Ned or Rob remain with him?"

"Rob was leading my horse and was to lodge at my uncle's with Joan and me. Ned was to stop with Clement at the Baptist's Head but my uncle's two men seemed anxious for his company. They were full of stories of bands of armed men who roamed the city streets, preying particularly on women, and my brother urged Ned to do as they asked. He could rejoin him later, Clement said. Besides, the inn was only a little way down the lane, within sight of where we left him." Alison dipped a fore-finger in the remains of her ale and drew a rough map on the table. "This is Thames Street," she said, "and this—" she made another damp line at right-angles to it—"is Crooked Lane, running down to the wharves and the river. Here, at the corner where we dropped him, is another inn called the Crossed Hands, and the Baptist's Head is a little further down on the opposite side. We could see the sign and the lanterns hung on the wall. It was only a few steps for him to go and we did not wait. My uncle's men were anxious to be home before curfew and I think we were all looking forward to our beds. I leaned out of the coach to wave goodbye. Clement was standing, huddled inside his cloak, immediately beneath a torch fixed high up, near an upstairs window of the Crossed Hands inn. He waved back, then made an impatient gesture to speed us on our way. I drew the curtains of the coach and settled back into my seat for the remainder of the journey. I remember remarking to Joan how tired I was and that I should be glad to be safely indoors. It was a wild night and I recall how the torches guttered when my uncle and aunt came out to greet us. Ned returned at once to Crooked Lane and the Baptist's Head." Her voice caught in her throat. "But he never found Clement. He wasn't there. Thomas Prynne said he'd never arrived."

CHAPTER
4

 Into the silence which followed her words came a second roll of thunder. I had not noticed the lightning flash which preceded it, so absorbed had I been by Alison Weaver's story. In my mind's eye I could envisage quite plainly the figure of her brother as she had last seen him, huddled in his cloak against the driving rain, illuminated by the flickering torchlight of the Crossed Hands inn, with so few steps between himself and safety. The Baptist's Head was within sight, Thomas Prynne, his father's old friend, waiting to welcome him, a posset of warm ale already brewing on the fire . . . But Clement Weaver had never arrived.

The noise of the thunder made us all jump. Marjorie, coming to her senses, realized that the rain was driving in through the open door and with a cluck of annoyance, got up to shut it, stirring the pot of stew at the same time. "All this talk," she grumbled. "I'm forgetting my duties. A wonder the meat hasn't stuck to the bottom and burned."

Neither Alison nor I paid her much attention. "Was it truly necessary," I asked, "for Ned to go with you? Even without him, there would still have been three grown men protecting you and your maid."

"You forget," Alison replied patiently, "that it was a very dangerous time just then. The Earl of Warwick had brought King Henry out of the Tower and proclaimed him rightful King again. The sanctuaries were overflowing with King Edward's followers, and there were many not even in sanctuary, but hiding in the city. And it was only a matter of weeks since the execution of the Earl of Worcester. My uncle told me he had never seen the Londoners in such a restless, feverish state of excitement. He said the number of crimes was rising daily."

I remembered that even we, in our seclusion at Glastonbury, had heard some rumors of the terrible mob violence which had occurred in London at the execution of King Edward's Constable. The Earl of Worcester had been nicknamed the Butcher of England, after he had once had rebels' bodies as well as their heads impaled on stakes, and had been hated by the people ever since. But even that, had said our informant, an itinerant friar, could not wholly explain the ferocity of the Londoners, who had all but succeeded in tearing the prisoner to pieces on his way to the scaffold. It was the only occasion the friar could recall when an execution had had to be postponed while captive and gaolers took refuge for a night in the Fleet prison. So I supposed there had been sufficient reason for John Weaver to be concerned about the safety of his niece, and to have alarmed his men enough for them to have talked Ned into going with them. That way, they were not solely responsible for the safety of their master's guest. Rob, in any case, was to stay with Alison and her maid.

The housekeeper busied herself with making a junket. "Your father will be home soon," she remarked, nodding at Alison. "It's nearly supper-time."

I was surprised. The four hours since noon and my meeting with Marjorie Dyer at the High Cross had passed so swiftly that I might almost have thought her mistaken had I not been able to hear the Vespers bell ringing from one of the nearby churches. Three hours to Compline, I thought automatically.

"He won't be here yet awhile." Alison glanced at me. "Well, that's the story."

I frowned. "You say that no one but your father and your brother himself knew how much money he was carrying. That may be true, but surely everyone concerned with the venture must have been aware that your brother had money on him, and a substantial sum at that, if it was known that you were going to London to buy your bride-clothes."

"What are you suggesting?" Alison's voice rose sharply. "That a member of this household, or my uncle's household, was in some way responsible for Clement's disappearance?"

"Yes, are you suggesting that?" Marjorie echoed, her face bright red with indignation.

I realized guiltily that my thoughts had indeed been

straying in that direction. Supposing Ned or Rob or either of John Weaver's men were hand-in-glove with one of the many cut-throat bands of thieves and pickpockets who roamed the London streets, and had given their fellow criminals prior warning . . . But no! How could they, when no one could have foreseen the exact circumstances of Clement Weaver's arrival; the casting of his horse's shoe, which prevented his riding straight into the court-yard of the Baptist's Head and the safety of Thomas Prynne's welcoming arms. Nor could anyone have fore-told that Ned would not be with him. The two women were right to be angry. I had not allowed myself time to consider the implications of my question.

"I'm sorry," I said. "It was a foolish conclusion to jump to."

"And a false one!" I wondered for a moment if Alison were about to withdraw her offer of a lodging for the night, but she went on: "I didn't like the look of that place, the Crossed Hands inn."

"You think . . . You think it might have had some-thing to do with your brother's disappearance?"

She chewed her bottom lip. "I've no reason for say-ing so," she admitted reluctantly, after a pause. "My fa-ther and uncle made inquiries there, when they were searching for Clement, but the landlord and servants swore they had heard and seen nothing. There was no cause to doubt them. Nor was there anything to suggest that they were in any way connected with what had hap-pened to Clement."

"But you think they might have been lying?"

Alison shrugged. "I just felt there was something a

little sinister about the place, that's all. I'm probably being silly."

I thought privately that she probably was. She had seen the inn under the most unfavorable conditions, late in the afternoon, in near darkness and pouring rain, when she was hungry and tired. And she had inevitably associated it with her brother's disappearance. It was the last time that she had seen him, standing beneath the flaring torchlight . . . Once again, the picture sprang, fully formed, into my mind.

I hesitated for a moment before putting my final question. It was a delicate one, and I felt for the second time that I could be putting my night's billet by the kitchen fire at risk. Nevertheless, in spite of what Marjorie had said to me earlier, I felt compelled to ask it, if only for my own satisfaction. Wherever I slept, I should sleep the sounder for having tied up the loose ends of this problem. I have always disliked loose ends.

"Is there any reason at all," I began cautiously, "why your brother would have . . . might have . . . ? What I am trying to say is . . ."

Alison Weaver interrupted me. Her voice was like ice. "You're asking me if Clement would have robbed his own father? The answer to that is no."

I knew I should have left it there, but I persisted. I had to convince myself that she was telling the truth. "A great deal of money was involved. Young men have been known to succumb to sudden temptation."

I expected her to fly into a rage, but, somewhat to my surprise, she answered my impertinence calmly enough. Calmly, but, I have to admit, coldly. "Clement and I love our father. He has never given us reason to do otherwise. My brother, particularly, has always been close to him and will take over the business when my father is too old to continue. There has never been any dissension between them.''

"I've already told you that," the housekeeper reproached me.

"I know." I was somewhat shamefaced. I could see she was hurt by my inability to accept her word, but I had needed confirmation. Alison had spoken with heartfelt sincerity and there had been no hesitation about her reply.

The silence grew around us, holding us, enclosing us. There was nothing more to be said. Like Marjorie, like Alison, for all that she had spoken of her brother just now as if he were still alive, I was convinced that Clement Weaver had been murdered. Whether his attackers were connected with the Crossed Hands inn or no—and I thought not—he had been set upon, robbed and killed that wet November afternoon last year and his body disposed of. In the fading light it would have been the work of a moment to slip a knife between his ribs. There would have been no sound, no cry, to carry as far as the Baptist's Head and alert his waiting friend. And even if he had managed to call out, it was doubtful if he could have been heard above the noise of the rain. No, when all the facts were assembled, the answer was still the same; the simple answer, the obvious answer. Clement Weaver had been one of the hundreds of men and women who were murdered each year for the money which they might, or might not, be carrying. The world was a violent and dangerous place, as Abbot Selwood had warned me when I left the Abbey to seek my fortune, outside the safety of its walls.

The three of us were so engrossed, each in his or her own thoughts, that no one heard the opening and shutting of the street door. The first any of us knew of the Alderman's return was his voice raised in question.

"Alison? Marjorie? Are you there?"

"God's Body!" Marjorie turned from her junket-making with a flurry of skirts. "Your father's home, and not a plate on the table. And gone supper-time by now, I shouldn't wonder!" She waved an agitated hand at me. "Out of my way, you! You've kept me gossiping too long." She turned to Alison. "You'd best go and greet him."

But the girl was already moving towards the door, calling out: "I'm here, Father! Supper will be on the table presently." The kitchen door shut behind her.

"Presently, is it?" Marjorie grumbled. "It'll be more like half an hour before I'm ready."

She bustled about, much faster than I should have expected, given her bulk and the bad legs of which she had complained. She loaded plates and knives and pewter beakers on to a tray of beaten copper which she then bore off to the parlor, where the family took their meals. Afraid of hindering her, I resumed my seat beside the fire and waited patiently until she should have time to spare for me again. A few moments later she was back, muttering furiously.

"Here's Master Burnett returned with the Alderman and asked to share the meal. Am I ever given warning?

No, I'm not! I'm just one of the servants as far as they're concerned." She seized hold of the ladle, a piece of cloth wound around her hand, and gave the stew another vigorous stir. "You'd never think, would you, that I'm the Alderman's cousin?"

So that was it. She was a poor relation of the Weaver family, which explained the peculiar relationship which seemed to exist between her and Alison; on one hand that of mistress and servant, on the other that of family friend.

The back door opened and two men came in, both short and stocky, with the heavy, lantern-jawed faces, swarthy skin and dark hair which are prevalent among the inhabitants of Bristol. There has been much intermarrying over the centuries between them and the people of southern Wales, and the Celtic coloring has predominated over that of the Saxon. One man, the smaller of the two, was obviously the elder, and I guessed him to have something more than thirty summers. The younger was probably about my age. I suspected that they were Ned and Rob, the Alderman's menservants.

"It's no good looking for your victuals yet awhile," Marjorie scolded them. "I'm late as it is, and Master William come for his supper, and no warning. Out of my way, you great oafs! Sit by the fire, with the chapman."

The older man shrugged and muttered, "I'll be back later," making his way once more into the garden, where the storm had blown itself out, stopping as suddenly as it had started. The sun had reappeared from behind the clouds, and I could sniff the sweet-smelling herbs and grasses. The younger man, however, did as he was bidden and came to sit by me, dragging another stool, covered with the same green and red cloth, out of its corner.

He nodded briefly, regarding me askance, as though uncertain as to what I was doing there. "My name's Roger," I said, offering my hand.

"Ned Stoner," he grunted, squeezing my fingers until the bones cracked.

So this was the young man who had returned to Crooked Lane to find Clement Weaver missing; vanished from the face of the earth as though he had never been. I took covert stock of him and liked what I saw. He was somewhat slovenly in his general appearance; there were grease and food stains down the front of his jerkin, a tear in the left knee of his thick woolen hose and his leather shoes were scuffed and dusty. But he had an honest, open face and a particularly friendly smile, which tended every now and then to broaden into what I can only describe as a joyous grin. He obviously loved life and I could no more have suspected him of harming a hair of anyone's head than I could have suspected myself. He knew nothing about his young master's disappearance, I decided.

An arbitrary decision, you might say, and you'd be right. But you have to remember that I was green in those days; a callow youth who knew nothing about the world, but thought he knew everything. In the long years between then and now, I've learned more than once that you can't judge a book by its cover.

Alison reappeared in the kitchen doorway.

"It's no good looking for food on the table yet," Marjorie snapped at her, putting a pan of plovers' eggs on the fire to boil. "I can't work miracles."

The girl ignored her and crooked a finger at me. "My father wants to see you."

There was an astonished silence, while the three of

us, the housekeeper, Ned and myself, gaped at her stupidly. It was Marjorie who found her tongue first. "Why would the Alderman want to see a chapman?"

Alison raised eyebrows which I noticed, for the first time, had been inexpertly plucked in order to emulate the almost non-existent eyebrows of great and fashionable ladies. "If that were your business, Marjorie, I'd tell you." She looked at me. "Well," she asked impatiently, "are you coming?"

I rose to my feet, glancing apologetically at the housekeeper, and smoothed down my shabby doublet with awkward hands. I had considered the possibility that the Alderman would rescind his daughter's promise of a night's free lodging, but not that he would wish to do so face to face. After all, it was not I who had broken the rules of his household.

I followed Alison into the hall, off which parlor, kitchen and buttery all opened. In spite of my trepidation, I noticed that although the windows giving on to Broad Street had wooden shutters below, the top halves were made of glass. Nowadays we think far less of glass in private houses, but it was quite a new thing in England then, and very expensive. The Alderman was plainly a man of substance. The doorposts and ends of the roof-beams had birds and faces and flowers carved on them, and were painted red and gold. There was a big, equally ornate cupboard in one corner, in which the family silver and pewter were displayed, and two carved armchairs one on each side of the fireplace. The Alderman was seated in the larger of these, his future son-in-law in the other.

Alderman Weaver was a florid, thickset man with eyes the same green-flecked hazel as his daughter's, and dark hair already going thin on top. He wore it in a style long gone out of fashion, cropped short above his ears, with a few strands plastered carefully across his pinkly shining pate. His long, fur-trimmed gown was also of a previous age, with a hood attached to it, as had been fashionable earlier in the century. I say this with hindsight, you understand. I had been too short a time out in the world to understand then what was modish.

Mind you, I had a pretty good notion when I looked at Alison Weaver's betrothed. William Burnett's auburn hair hung to his shoulders, with a thick fringe cut so low across his eyes that he could barely see. His smooth-skinned face was clean-shaven, a fact which immediately made me conscious of my own day-old stubble of beard, and his fiercely padded doublet, half purple, half red, with its narrow belted waist, was indecently short, revealing a codpiece decorated with tassels. But the chief point of focus was his shoes, made of soft scarlet leather and with toes so long that they had to be fastened with thin gold chains around his knees. These toe-pieces were known as pikes and made walking difficult. A few years earlier, a papal Bull had limited pikes to two inches in length, on pain of a papal cursing. But English cordwainers had ignored this edict on the grounds that "the Pope's curse would not hurt a fly," and continued to make shoes in this fantastical fashion.

I could hear the Alderman's voice as I emerged from the kitchen.

"If King Edward wins the coming struggle, there will be fines levied, and they'll be heavy. I warned the rest of the Council against letting the Frenchwoman into the city, but they wouldn't listen. Some of the burgesses have always been for the House of Lancaster. A grave mistake, in my view, to take sides openly. There have been too many swings of the pendulum, these past few years, to be free with one's opinions. Wait and see, is my motto, and a sound one. We could have made some excuse to bar the gates. Plague always offers a valid reason. They won't make the same foolish mistake at Gloucester, you mark my words. Up there, they have a strong sense of self-preservation."

William Burnett grunted indifferently, too busy smoothing the dark purple satin of one sleeve to have much interest in the Alderman's worries. Alison regarded him with admiration.

The Alderman suddenly became aware of my presence and transferred his attention from his future son-in-law to me, looking me over with shrewd appraisal. I stood there for a moment or two, the subject of his scrutiny, waiting for the order to get out of his house. But none came; and after a silence which seemed to stretch unbearably, he remarked: "So you're the chapman my daughter has been telling me about. She says you can read and write." He nodded thoughtfully to himself. "That could be useful."

CHAPTER
5

 I was unsure how my skills of reading and writing could be useful to Alderman Weaver, so I maintained a diplomatic and not unhopeful silence. At least it looked as though my night's lodging might be safe, after all. He had not reacted like a man who was about to turn me out into the street.

After another pause, he went on painfully: "Alison also tells me that you know about . . . about my son's . . . disappearance." I nodded gently. I could see that the subject caused him great distress. He swallowed hard and one hand played restlessly with the trimming of budge which edged his gown. "I don't . . . approve of gossiping with strangers, of making every jack-in-the-hedge privy to my family's affairs. But in your case my daughter may have been wise to make an exception." I was still in the dark and glanced sideways at Alison, but she looked as mystified as I was myself. The Alderman continued: "Do your travels often take you to London?"

"I—er—" I cleared my throat. "I've never been there." I hurried on: "But I intend to do so. I haven't been on the road very long, you understand. Mistress Alison must have told you that until recently I was a novice with the Benedictines at Glastonbury. But London is my goal. A man can make his fortune there, if he's clever."

William Burnett roused himself from his enraptured contemplation of the tassels on his codpiece and gave me a lofty smile.

"You fancy yourself as another Richard Whittington, do you? You won't make that sort of fortune selling needles and thread and ribbons in the Cheap. Besides—" his condescension was overpowering—"Whittington was, after all, the son of a gentleman."

Alderman Weaver waved him to silence with an impatient hand. "That's neither here nor there." He turned back to me. "The point is, boy, when you do get to London, I want you to keep your eyes and ears open for any whisper as to the fate of my son. You can mix with people I can't in my position. Oh, I'm able to question them, but that's no good. If they've anything to conceal, they'll lie faster than a dog can run. But with you, they'll talk openly. You'll overhear conversations to which I could never be privy. So, if you hear anything, anything at all, which you think might be of value—the slightest indication as to what happened to Clement—go to my old friend, Thomas Prynne at the sign of the Baptist's

Head in Crooked Lane and he'll see to it that I get your message. Well? Will you do that for me?"

"Yes. Yes, of course," I said, wondering if the poor man realized that he was clutching at straws. But what else did he have to clutch at? He couldn't just sit back and tamely accept that his only son was dead.

"And as you can read and write," he went on, "you have an advantage. You may see something . . . read something . . ." This was not just clutching at straws, but at straws on the wind.

"If I can find out anything at all," I promised, "I shall go at once to your friend Thomas Prynne. But I may not be in London for many months yet. I have only my own two legs, and my living to earn as I go. Villages and hamlets away from the main tracks are my best source of livelihood; distant places, where the inhabitants are far from the nearest market."

I could see that the Alderman was disappointed. His shoulders sagged and he looked dispirited. He had imagined me being in London within a couple of weeks.

"Well . . ." He drummed with his fingers on the arm of his chair. "Whenever you get there, you would still oblige me by keeping a lookout." He made an effort to sound cheerful and my heart warmed to him. He patently wasn't a man to vent his spleen on underlings for something that was not their fault. I could see why his children were fond of him. Moreover, he hadn't sent them away to be brought up in other people's households, like so many of his kind. He had kept them with him and showed them affection; not a very common trait, except among the poor. He smiled and nodded my dismissal, adding: "My daughter says she has offered you a bed by the kitchen fire for the night. If you want it, you're welcome to stay."

I mumbled my thanks and returned to the kitchen, where Marjorie Dyer was getting ready to carry the pot of stew into the parlor. There was also a meat pie, the plovers' eggs and a dish piled high with fritters, side by side with a bowl of almonds and raisins. The junket was still only half-set, but Marjorie had produced a plate of fruit tarts to round off the meal. If this were supper, I wondered what they had eaten for dinner.

When she returned from serving in the parlor, she, Ned Stoner and I sat at the kitchen table and applied ourselves to our own meal. There was more of the stew and goat's milk cheese, together with black bread and spring vegetables from the garden. Marjorie also found from somewhere, with a conspiratorial nod and wink, a plate of pastry doucettes, filled with egg yolks, cream, saffron, and sweetened with honey. Of the other man, Rob, there was still no sign.

"What did the Alderman want you for?" Marjorie asked, once she had blunted the edge of her hunger. And when I explained, she sighed gustily and wiped her mouth on a corner of her sleeve. "Poor man." She echoed my own thoughts with uncanny precision. "Clutching at straws. He can't accept that Master Clement is dead."

I turned to Ned. "When you got back to the Crossed Hands inn that night, were there any signs of a struggle?"

He crammed his mouth with a spoonful of stew and answered thickly: "It was raining." After a few seconds' mastication, he added the one word: "Hard."

"You mean any telltale marks would have been washed away?"

" 'S right." He took a massive bite of cheese which effectually prevented any further conversation with him for at least two minutes.

When he had finally cleared his mouth, and before he could fill it again, I inquired urgently: "There was nothing at all? Nothing, for instance, ripped from your master's clothing? A button? A buckle? A scrap of material perhaps?"

Ned stared at me, frowning. He plainly considered me mad. "It was raining," he repeated. "I didn't stand rakin' about in the mud. Besides—" he shrugged his shoulders—"I wasn't lookin' fer anything, was I? I thought me young master safe at the Baptist's Head. 'Tweren't till I got there, I knew he was missing."

A sudden thought struck me. "What about your master's baggage? Did he have that with him?"

Ned considered the question with as much gravity as if I had asked him to explain some abstruse mathematical theorem. One hand, none too clean and with black-rimmed fingernails, hovered impatiently in the vicinity of his mouth, holding a spoonful of stew. At last, he nodded. "His saddlebags were in the coach with Miss Alison, but Rob and I lifted them out fer 'im and put 'em down on the road. I remember seeing them by his feet as we rode away. He only had a little distance to carry 'em." This last was added somewhat defensively, as though Ned were afraid of being accused of failing in his duty. The stew disappeared into the wide, gaping cavern of his mouth. He champed slowly and with satisfaction.

"And they were never found, either?"

"Not likely, is it? Emptied and dropped in the Thames." Marjorie pushed the plate of pastry doucettes towards me. "Have one of these and stop fretting. You're worrying at this thing like a dog with a rat." She lowered her voice, leaning across the table to clasp my hand. "Look, lad, forget it. Master Clement's gone and there's nothing you or anyone can do about it. He fell among thieves, like the man in the Bible. It's natural enough that the Alderman should want to think otherwise; that some day, somewhere, Clement will turn up again, but it's not going to happen, and in his heart of hearts, he knows it. If you want to salve your conscience when you finally get to London, you can ask a few questions at the Crossed Hands inn, but don't waste your time doing more than that. There's nothing to find out, and sooner or later my master is going to have to accept the truth."

Ned nodded in mute agreement, having just refilled his mouth with a whole doucette, the honey and cream running down his chin. Reluctantly, because I found the problem intriguing, I, too, was forced to agree. What Marjorie said made sense. All the same, some nagging worry, which refused to be pinpointed, hovered at the back of my mind.

After supper was finished and cleared away, I went out into the garden. Beyond its walls, the city was quieter, free at last of the clatter of horses' hooves and the continual braying of trumpets. Presumably, Margaret of Anjou and her troops had gone, continuing their progress northward. Bristol was free of her unwanted military presence and could settle back, in uneasy calm, to await the outcome of the Queen's clash with King Edward. Where and how it would take place, and who would win, were still unknown factors, and perhaps not much thought about that fine May evening. Life, after all, had to go on.

It was beautiful in the garden. The dappled shadows inched their way across the beds of herbs and flowers, and a bird sang lustily in the branches of the pear tree. The sky was a clear, translucent blue, washed clean by the rain, and promising yet another fine day tomorrow. Not an evening to be thinking of violence and death, and it was easy to forget the fate of Clement Weaver. But Marjorie was right. There was nothing to be done and the Alderman was asking the impossible. I had no wish, I told myself, to be drawn into his affairs and would do well to stay out of them. I went into the privy and closed the door behind me.

When I emerged, Rob was coming in at the garden gate, and had plainly been drinking. He had taken his supper, mostly liquid, I guessed, at the inn at the end of the street and was now rolling slightly from side to side. He grinned inanely when he saw me, before pushing past into the warmth of the kitchen. I heard Marjorie's voice upraised reproachfully, but by the time I went indoors myself, Rob was already curled up by the side of the fire, his head resting on one arm, fast asleep and snoring loudly.

It was Rob's snoring which roused me in the middle of the night. I raised my head slowly from where it rested on my pack, and stared around the shadowed kitchen.

The fire was burning low, but not yet out, and there was no light filtering between the slats of the shutters. I could make out Ned's humped form, where he lay huddled in one corner, but he made no sound except for his quiet, regular breathing. Rob, on the other hand, snorted and whistled and tossed restlessly from side to side, his mouth wide open to emit gusts of stinking breath. Even from where I was lying, I could smell the stench of sour ale.

I eased myself into a sitting position, stretching my cramped limbs. I must have been sleeping awkwardly because I had pains all down the back of my left leg and a tingling sensation in my left arm. I suddenly felt wide awake, which was something that happened frequently, and I knew the reason for it. It was about that time of two hours past midnight when I had been used to dragging my unwilling body from the dorter to the choir for the singing of Matins and Lauds.

I lay down again and tried to sleep, but my eyes refused to stay closed. I stared into the heart of the crumbling logs, where a fringe of thick grey ash trembled in a draft from the door. A fairy world of caverns and grottoes opened up before me, and each time a bead of resin caught fire, a flame would spurt, blue and yellow, up the chimney. A shadow moved, and the kitchen cat, sleek, fat and purring, came to make his bed beside me, but daring me to touch him with a fiercely gleaming eye. He had evidently eaten well because he was licking his lips and exuded contentment. There was one mouse or rat the less to raid the flour and corn bins.

Gradually, my eyelids drooped and I began drifting towards the edge of sleep . . .

I was standing outside the Crossed Hands inn: I could see the sign of the two crossed hands quite plainly.

It was raining hard and my jerkin clung soggily to my back. Above my head, fixed high on the wall near a shuttered window, a torch hissed and flared in its sconce, the flames torn sideways by the driving wind. At my feet were two saddlebags. I bent down to pick them up, all my movements hampered and leaden, as though I were moving through water. But just as my hand reached to grab them, something stopped me. I straightened slowly, peering into the darkness. Someone or something was coming towards me out of the murk, but strain my eyes as I might, I could make out no features. I only knew that whoever or whatever it was, it was evil . . .

I woke with a start, jerking upright and bathed in sweat. Rob was snoring even louder, but apart from that, all was quiet in the kitchen. The cat was cleaning itself before bedding down for the rest of the night among the rushes. The rushes themselves smelled stale. Marjorie would no doubt change them in the morning. I tried to keep my mind on such mundane things in order to stop myself shaking. The dream was still so vivid in my mind that I could sense the lingering aura of evil and it took all my strength of will not to wake one of the others.

After a while I lay down again, but this time sleep eluded me completely. The truth was, I did not want to lose consciousness in case the dream returned. The fire was nothing now but a dim glow on the hearthstones and the room was growing cold. Yet still there was no slackening of the darkness and there were many hours to go before dawn.

Above my head, a board creaked, once, twice, three times. At first I thought it was nothing more than the beams settling, the way they do in houses at night when it begins to get chilly. But then I realized that someone was moving about, padding across the room directly overhead. At any other time, in any other circumstances, I should have taken no notice. There are many reasons why people leave their beds at night, and it was none of my business. But because my nerves were stretched to breaking-point, because I needed the reassurance that someone else in the house was awake besides myself, because I needed to shake off the effects of my nightmare and, above all, because I have always suffered, and still do, from an insatiable curiosity, I got silently to my feet and tiptoed across to the kitchen door. Carefully lifting the latch, while keeping a wary eye on my sleeping companions, I stepped through into the darkness of the hall beyond. All was quiet now, and when one of the wall hangings bellied in the draft, I nearly jumped out of my skin. Getting a grip on myself, I moved stealthily towards the staircase spiraling upwards into the gloom of the second story, and set a foot cautiously on the lowest tread. To my relief, it did not creak and I crept up, cat-footed, until my head was on a level with the first landing. A door into one of the bedchambers was standing ajar, and as my eyes were by now thoroughly accustomed to the darkness, I was able to make out the outline of a handsome four-poster bed. No great feat of deduction was needed to know that this must be the Alderman's room, nor that it was probably he who had been moving about.

I suddenly realized that if anyone were to find me there, stealing around the house like a thief in the night, it would look bad for me. And rightly so. I had kindly been offered shelter, and was abusing the Alderman's hospitality by spying on him and his family. And for no good reason; nothing that I could even explain to myself.

Yet I made no attempt to go, lowering my weight to sit on a stair and continuing to peer over the top one. After a moment or two, there came the whisper of voices and then another noise which sounded like kissing. Seconds later, Marjorie Dyer, in a billowing white nightshift, appeared in the doorway like a voluminous ghost and softly closed the bedchamber door behind her. She tip-toed past me, only inches from my face, and vanished up the second flight of stairs to her own room in the attics.

The blood rushed into my face, and I cursed myself roundly for a Peeping Tom. What more natural than that the widowed Alderman should find comfort of a sort with his housekeeper, who was also his cousin? I felt deeply ashamed of myself and began easing my way downstairs. How could I have been so foolish as to imagine that anything sinister was happening? I blamed the nightmare, although it was difficult to understand why I had been so frightened. It now seemed nothing more than an unpleasant dream.

Affairs in the kitchen were exactly as I had left them; Ned still sound asleep in his corner, sucking his thumb; Rob drunkenly snoring. Neither had awakened to miss me, and I resumed my place near the almost dead fire, resting my head on my pack and wrapping myself in my cloak for warmth. I had no trouble this time in dropping off, with no fears of my dream recurring, and was once more on the borderline of sleep when I found myself wide awake again. The thing which had been puzzling me, nagging away at the back of my mind all evening, had suddenly pushed its way to the fore. If Clement

Weaver had been murdered by footpads for his money and possessions, as seemed most likely, why had his attackers bothered to remove the body? Having ransacked his pockets and seized his saddle-bags, why had they not simply left him lying there, on the roadway? Why impede their escape by carrying a corpse along with them?

The more I thought about it, the less sense it made. Swiftness of hand and fleetness of foot were surely the essence of highway robbery. An ordinary pickpocket or footpad, having once accomplished the deed, would have melted away into the darkness; back into that criminal world whence he had come, with its maze of alleyways and taverns and brothels . . .

My head spun with weariness. It seemed a long time since I had left Whitchurch early the previous morning. My head ached and I felt I was becoming obsessed by something which was not my problem. I had taken to the open road for the freedom it offered; to live for myself and not to become involved with things that did not concern me. But if I was to achieve this desirable state, I should have to learn to be less curious. "Nosey" was the harsher word my mother had always used for it.

"You must learn, my son, to keep that nose of yours out of other people's business."

I resolved sleepily to be off at the crack of dawn, before anyone else was stirring. I would shake Bristol's dust off my feet and, with luck be at the village of Keynsham by dinner-time.

PART II

September 1471
Canterbury

CHAPTER
6

 The Saint's tomb gleamed with hundreds of precious stones, so thickly encrusted that the gold in which they were set was well-nigh invisible. Above the tomb hung St. Thomas's hair shirt, and, to the left, was a small spring which had been seen to run with milk and blood. In the crypt behind it was one of the swords which had killed the Archbishop; while in the choir, adorned with yet more jewels and large creamy pearls, stood a picture of the Virgin, which, so it was said, had talked with the Saint during his lifetime. The enormous ruby, the Regale of France, given by King Louis, seventh of his name, glowed like liquid fire, and the candlelight struck sparks from the sapphires and diamonds.

There were other relics, too, here in this great cathedral where Thomas à Becket had been martyred three centuries ago; the nails and right arm of St. George, some of the Holy Thorns which had pierced Christ's brow, a tooth of John the Baptist, a finger of St. Urban, and the upper lip of one of the Murdered Innocents. Even I, coming so recently from Glastonbury, the oldest Christian shrine in England, was overwhelmed by the sanctity of the place, and by the awestruck devotion of the many pilgrims around me.

I, too, had travelled the last part of my journey by the Pilgrims' Way, joining it after I left Southampton, where I had gone to replenish my stock of merchandise from some of the ships just put into port, and from the market in High Street near St. Lawrence's church. By purchasing in bulk from the stall-holders I could get things cheap, then add the necessary penny to make my profit when selling to outlying villagers and hamlet-dwellers. It was a rougher life than I had anticipated when I first set out on my travels. I had slept under as many hedges and in drafty barns as I had in the slightly less spartan conditions of an abbey or a priory guest-house. Yet I wouldn't have changed it for all the safety of four permanent walls, even though I knew I had so far had the best of the weather and that the winter was still to come.

"You'll change your tune, my lad," a fellow traveller had said to me one evening, "when the roads are blocked with snow or slippery with ice, and the womenfolk won't venture out of doors." He was an unfrocked priest, turned out of his parish for some misdemeanor and forced to beg for his living from door to door. It was a bad night, I remember, cold and wet, and we had taken refuge in somebody's byre just to get out of the rain. If the owner had discovered us, no doubt we should have been turned out into the elements, but the cows had been milked and had raised no alarm, merely chewing the cud contentedly and regarding us with solemn, incurious eyes.

But even under those conditions, and with my companion's pessimism sounding in my ears, I had no regrets. "I'll deal with winter when it comes," I said, taking bread and cheese from the pouch at my waist and sharing it with my doleful ex-priest. We cheered one another up through a night of fitful slumber by exchanging scurrilous anecdotes about the Church and churchmen.

But now, standing on the hallowed ground of Canterbury, I felt ashamed of my ribaldry, and something like nostalgia for my former life momentarily swept over me. I wanted to be one again with the brothers at Glastonbury and to feel assured of Christ's love. I looked into the face of the painted Virgin, searching for some sign of divine approval for the decision I had taken to leave the Abbey.

"Holy Mother, pray for me, now and in the hour of my death." I crossed myself, at the same moment becoming aware of the kneeling figure on my right, draped from head to toe in black and with a heavy veil concealing her face. To one side of, and slightly behind, this suppliant, whoever she was, a young girl wriggled uncomfortably, her knees pressed against the cold stone. She, too, was dressed in mourning, but it was plain and unadorned with any gold cross or jet rosary, such as hung about the woman's neck. Obviously, they were mistress and maid.

From somewhere, a draft stirred the woman's veil, and I was immediately transported back to Bristol, that warm May day almost five months ago when I had seen Anne Neville, together with Margaret of Anjou, riding along Corn Street. Then, they had been mother and daughter-in-law: now, the fortunes of both had been irrevocably changed. For the clash of arms which everyone expected had in fact taken place only two days later at Tewkesbury, and King Edward had been victorious. Margaret's son and Anne Neville's young husband, Edward of Lancaster, had been killed during the battle, whatever our present so-called historians might tell you to the contrary. He was not murdered afterwards by Richard of Gloucester, nor was his father; although Henry Plantagenet was undoubtedly put to death in the Tower, on the orders of the King, however much Edward and his Council would have wished us to believe that the poor man died of "pure displeasure and melancholy." Margaret of Anjou was at this time a prisoner of the King, while her erstwhile daughter-in-law had been restored to her sister, Isabel, and was living in the Duke of Clarence's household as an honored guest.

Here again, I feel I must stress that I was not then as knowledgeable of events which were happening in the larger world as my narrative would suggest, although I naturally gathered stray pieces of information along the way; particularly those of such grave importance as the outcome of the battle at Tewkesbury. And if I had remained ignorant of it before, I should certainly have learned of it in Canterbury, where they were still talking of the splendor of King Edward's summer visit, when he had come to render thanks at St. Thomas's shrine not only for his victory, but also for the birth of his son, born in Westminster sanctuary during his exile.

Remembering these things also prompted recollection of the Weavers, to whom, I must admit, I had given little thought in the intervening months. The episode now seemed dreamlike and distant, something which had happened a very long time ago and to another person. I recalled guiltily my promise to the Alderman to make inquiries concerning his son when I reached London; but somehow, although the capital still beckoned, and remained my goal, I had not yet reached there. However, it was my avowed intention to go when I left Canterbury; but whether, on arrival, I should keep my word and search for Clement Weaver was a different matter. It now seemed not only impossible, but fruitless; a waste of time which I could ill afford. It was ten months since his disappearance, and in any case, what was there to find out which had not been discovered already? The more I thought about it, the more foolish seemed my promise to his father. I was sure that after this lapse of time, the Alderman would absolve me.

The woman beside me had risen from her knees and was making preparations to leave, motioning to her attendant as she did so. The girl caught my eye, pulling down the corners of her mouth in a comic grimace of resignation, indicating that her mistress was not the easiest of people to deal with. Indeed, the woman was fussing peevishly with the folds of her gown, smoothing and arranging them with uneasy, fluttering hands, before joining the throng of other pilgrims making their way out of the choir. The girl, following obediently, turned to smile at me across her shoulder, then was swallowed up by the press. She left me with the impression of a tiptilted nose, bright blue eyes fringed with jet-black lashes, and dark, curling hair, judging by the tendrils which strayed from beneath her hood. Her skin was pale, made even more pallid by the black clothes she was wearing. Her demeanor suggested natural high spirits with difficulty suppressed, and there had been more than a hint of invitation in her manner. A pity, I reflected that I would be unable to take advantage of it, as we were unlikely to meet again. I knew neither her name nor that of her mistress, nor where they lived. Besides, I had my living to make and I must start knocking on doors.

There were rich pickings to be had in Canterbury, where the constant influx of pilgrims from all parts of the country meant an unceasing flow of money into the pockets of its citizens. It had more taverns and cookshops than any other town of its size that I had passed through. And more trouble, too: the streets were rarely quiet. There were frequent disputes between the clerical and secular interests of the town; between Mayor and Archbishop, layman and priest. They quarreled over water rights, the fishmarket, and whose authority it was to arrest wrongdoers; over ecclesiastical immunities and restraints of trade. It was nothing to see several brawls a day in the Canterbury streets, and it was not always simply fists which were used. I had been there less than a week, and already I had seen daggers drawn on more than one occasion. But then, the English have always been anticlerical in their attitudes. They have always resented the power of Rome.

Before leaving the cathedral, I returned once again to St. Thomas's tomb, kneeling before it in prayer. I meant to seek his intercession with the Heavenly Father for abandoning my religious life, but somehow, the words would not come. I was not truly contrite. Instead, I found myself wondering what it was like to have been dead for hundreds of years, while the flesh, the only house my soul knew, rotted from my bones. I remember folding my arms around my body, seeking the solid reassurance of skin and bone. I thought of lying in the cold earth while the centuries spun by above my head, but my imagination was unable to encompass it; that drift of years, weaving its ever-changing patterns, while I, once so alive, crumbled into dust . . .

Like a dog shaking water from its back, I shook off my gloomy thoughts and emerged some minutes later into the bustling streets and the fragile, crystalline beauty of the autumn day. The sky was a delicate blue, rinsed at the edges to a soft, pale green, and the September sunlight was warm on my back. I was alive and young. My life stretched before me. That was all that mattered.

I met the girl again the following day.

I had done well that morning, selling needles, thread, ribbons and a length of sarsanet, which I had picked up cheap in Southampton market, for nearly twice what I had paid for it. It was gone dinner-time and I was hungry, so I bought two meat pies from a cookshop and took them down to the banks of the Stour. I ate ravenously, wishing that I had treated myself to a third, then filled my leather bottle from the river, washing the food down with clear, cool water; Adam's ale, and on some occasions nearly as satisfying as the proper thing.

It was quieter outside the city walls, and I had chosen a secluded spot beneath some overhanging willows. Sunlight sparkled on the water and everywhere there was the sharp, dank smell of early autumn. A faint breeze rippled the grasses silver and green, and from where I sat, I could see the track leading to the West Gate. While I watched, two horsemen passed, their mounts blowing gustily through flaring nostrils, sweating hides glittering like polished metal, raking at the bits as they were reined in to a walk for their approach to the city. But that was the only sign of life that I saw for quite some time, and I began to nod. For the past few nights, since coming to Canterbury, I had slept in the dormitory of the Eastbridge Hospital, but my fellow guests had not made good bedmates. There was the inevitable snoring and wheezing one got in such places, but one man also suffered from a most distressing cough. No sooner, it seemed, had I dropped off to sleep, than he began hacking again, with a persistence that woke the rest of the room and sent one or two sleepless souls into a positive frenzy. Last night it had only been through my intervention that the poor man was saved from a beating. So, what with one thing and another, today I was tired, and before I knew what was happening, had begun to doze . . .

I was awakened by a hand on my shoulder and started upright, feeling very foolish. I felt even more foolish when I saw who it was: the young girl I had seen in the cathedral. I had thought her pretty yesterday, but this afternoon, without her mourning and dressed in a gown of home-dyed blue bysine, she looked even prettier. The color of the dress enhanced the blue of her eyes, and she had dragged off her hood to reveal a profusion of hair at once darker and curlier than I had imagined it.

The hood lay in her basket, along with flowers she had been gathering. These included the feathery, flat-topped heads of fleabane, and a quantity of the plant known as Ladies' Bedstraw, the bunched yellow heads clinging tightly to the long, pale stems. I remembered my mother collecting the selfsame plants; the first, burnt, gave off an acrid smoke which was death to fleas; the second she would boil, using the flowers to make dye, and extracting a substance from the stalks and leaves which could be used as a substitute for rennet.

The girl sat down beside me and took off her shoes and stockings, dipping her toes into the water. "Oh, that's nice," she breathed after a moment, turning to smile provocatively in my direction. "My feet are so hot and tired."

"It's a warm day," I said feebly, not knowing what other answer to make. I was not used to girls taking off their clothes in front of me, and found to my dismay that I was blushing.

She saw it, too, and gave a little crow of delight. "I do believe you're embarrassed, a great, well-set-up lad like you! Haven't you ever had a sweetheart?" She put her head on one side, consideringly. "No, I don't believe you have." She added, with a frankness which took my breath away: "You don't like boys, do you? Instead of girls, I mean."

"N—no, of course not!" I stammered hotly. I knew that such practices existed: they had existed among the monks, at Glastonbury, even though they were anathema to the Church and the punishment for sodomy was death.

(A great deal was overlooked by the Superiors of enclosed orders; whether wisely or not, who can tell? I am certainly not fit to sit in judgment.) No, it was not this which shocked me, but the revelation that a woman—and so young a woman—knew about these things and was, moreover, prepared to discuss them openly.

"That's all right, then," she said, wriggling backwards until she was right beside me, her little feet clear of the water and sparkling with a myriad drops. "Kiss me," she commanded, laughing again at my horrified expression. "Go on! I dare you!"

How was I to resist such an invitation? I bent my head to hers and did as she instructed. Her lips were soft and yielding and tasted faintly of salt. Immediately, she wound her arms around my neck and returned my kiss with passion. I fell back on the grass in sheer surprise, her thin, lithe body pressed urgently on top of me, and it was some time later that I sat up, disheveled and panting.

Which was how I came to lose my virginity at the advanced age of nineteen, when many of my sex could boast at least one, maybe two, bastard children. As for my companion, although I did not realize it at the time, she had nothing to lose.

As I adjusted my clothes, I said, appalled: "I don't even know your name."

She giggled. "It's Elizabeth, but most people call me Bess."

And for the second time that day I found myself remembering the Weavers. Clement Weaver's horse had been named Bess; the beast who had cast a shoe at Paddington. Once again, my conscience smote me.

"What's yours?" the girl asked. Then seeing my

blank stare, repeated the question impatiently. "What's yours? Your name, you stupid!"

"Oh! Yes . . . It's Roger."

"Roger the chapman, eh?" She leaned back on her elbows, quite at ease, as though what had just taken place was, for her, an everyday occurrence. And I think it probably was. No, not everyday, of course; that, perhaps, is an exaggeration. But I've met women like her on many occasions since, with the same sort of expression in their eyes; hungry and languorous both at once, dissatisfied, always searching for fulfillment. A few of them have been rather sad creatures, but Bess wasn't: she was vital and eager and, above all, inquisitive.

She began plying me with questions about how old I was, my family, where I came from; and before I knew it, I was again recounting my brief life's history. When it was finished, I said: "And what of you? Or are you a woman of mystery?"

She shook her head regretfully, the black curls dancing. "I wish I were. I should like to be very beautiful and very rich and live in London. And then the King would notice me and take me for his mistress."

"You'd be one of many, if all accounts are true," I put in drily—and was back in the Weavers' kitchen, listening to Marjorie Dyer. *The women all went wild about him. I reckon there were a few cuckolded husbands during that visit.*

Bess tossed her head. "One night with me and he'd forget the others." She had all the arrogant assurance of youth. "Anyway—" she shrugged—"it's not going to happen." Her chin jutted. "At least, not yet awhile. For now, I'll have to make do with the local lads and—" she gave me a glinting, sideways glance beneath lowered lashes—"the odd, handsome, passing stranger." She sighed. "No, for now I'll just have to go on serving my lady and pretend to be devoted to her interests."

"Who is your lady?" I asked. "And why is she in mourning?"

Bess answered the second question first. "She's in mourning for her father, who died last month. He was Sir Gregory Bullivant, a distant kinsman of Archbishop Bourchier. That's why the family are so prominent in Canterbury. I was lucky to get a place in my lady's household—or so my mother tells me."

"And her husband? Or is your lady not married?"

For the first time in our short acquaintance, Bess hesitated, looking around her at the golden haze of autumn which lay upon the sloping banks and trees; at the first shimmer of bronze and red touching the summer's green. After a moment's silence, her gaze shifted back to me.

"Oh, she's married. At least . . ." Again there was that hesitation before she continued: "My lady's husband is Sir Richard Mallory, a Knight of the Shire. They've been wed four years come Christmas, and very happily as far as anyone could see. Which made it all the more surprising, I suppose."

"Made what all the more surprising?" I asked, when she showed signs of sinking into some reverie of her own.

"What? Oh . . ." Bess sat forward suddenly, hugging her knees. "It was all the more surprising when he disappeared."

The silence was so profound that a moorhen thought it safe to leave her nest in the bank below us and take to the water. She was so close I could see the blue-green sheen of her breast and the rhythmic jerking of her head as she swam serenely onwards.

"What do you mean?" I asked Bess at last. "Has your lady's husband left her?"

Bess had closed her eyes against the sun, but now she lifted her heavy, almond-shaped lids to look at me. "In a manner of speaking, I suppose. He went to London two months since and never returned. My lady and my lady's father—Sir Gregory was still alive then—sent men to inquire after him, but no trace of Sir Richard was ever found. He left the Crossed Hands inn, where he had been lodging, for the journey home, and that was the last anyone saw or heard of him." She tilted her head inquiringly to one side. "Is anything the matter? You look as though you've seen a ghost."

Which, in a way, I suppose I had; the ghost of Clement Weaver.

Some people might call it coincidence, others the working of Divine Providence, that of all the girls I could have met in Canterbury I had fallen in with Bess. The reminders I had already had throughout the previous day and this inclined me to the second point of view, however reluctant I might be to admit it, and however hard I fought against the notion. Bess had been sent to me for a purpose other than that of proving my manhood.

If I had followed my own inclinations, I should have asked no more questions, made love to Bess again and gone on my way. But lying there among the sweet-smelling grasses, I felt that God was demanding something of me in return for His forgiveness for my having abandoned the religious life. I was to channel my natural curiosity into combating evil. There was no escape.

"Why did Sir Richard go to London?" I asked.

Bess edged forward and once more paddled her bare feet in the river. The thick, springing curls tumbled down her back and across her shoulders. "To pay his respects to King Edward and congratulate him on the victory at Tewkesbury. He had been ill of a fever when the King and his brothers came here earlier in the summer."

"Your master was for York, then?"

"Of course. I told you, my lady's family is distantly related to Cardinal Bourchier. And as the Archbishop is himself a kinsman of King Edward's mother, the Duchess of York, there has never been any conflict of loyalties in our house. My lady would never have married anyone who was for Lancaster."

"Who went with Sir Richard to London?"

Bess turned her head to peer at me over her shoulder. "You're very inquisitive."

"You've aroused my interest. A man who is happily married doesn't suddenly leave his wife." I repeated: "Who went with him?"

"Only his manservant, Jacob Pender. He vanished, along with my master."

I frowned. "Was this Jacob Pender married, too?"

She gave a little crow of laughter. "No. And vowed he never would be." Her eyes twinkled. "He was a good lover. More experienced than you."

I felt myself blush again. She really was incorrigible. She would find herself in trouble one of these days, if she wasn't careful, and be cast on to the street. But remonstrating with her would do no good. She wouldn't listen to me. And indeed, why should she?

"They stayed, you say, at the Crossed Hands inn?"

"So my lady told me. The owner is a cousin of a dependant of the Duke of Clarence, and with the Bullivants' royal connections . . ." She broke off, her eyes encouraging me to laugh with her at the pretensions and conceits of our betters.

But I was too preoccupied with my thoughts. "Would you know if this inn is situated in a place called Crooked Lane, off Thames Street?"

Bess wriggled round to face me, tucking her wet feet

beneath her skirt, regardless of the grass- and mudstains they were making.

"That's right. I've heard my lady mention it often enough since her husband's disappearance. Sir Gregory finally went himself in pursuit of his son-in-law—a fact which is generally held to have hastened his death—and they were discussing it the night before he left. I distantly recall my lady saying: 'Crooked Lane off Thames Street.' Why, do you know it?"

"I know of it," I answered slowly. "And of the Crossed Hands inn. So, Sir Gregory was unsuccessful." It was not a question as she had already told me the answer, and I went on: "Do you think you could persuade your lady to see me?"

"Why? What has it do with you?"

"I might have some information in which she would be interested. Oh, I don't know what's become of Sir Richard any more than you do, but I'd like to hear the story from her own lips."

"You'd like to hear . . ." Bess was beginning with an incredulous smile, but something in my face must have given her pause, because she stopped smiling and regarded me thoughtfully for several moments. "I might be able to persuade her," she agreed at last, "if, of course, I know the whole story and what it is you have to say."

I hesitated, but only for an instant. There was no reason why she should not know, and anyway, it was obvious that satisfied curiosity was the price of her cooperation. And I owed her something. I patted the grass beside me, where she had been sitting before edging nearer to the water. "Come here," I said, "and I'll tell you."

* * *

The manor house which had been the home of Sir Richard Mallory, and where his wife still lived, was a little way outside the city walls, south, on the Dover road. I approached it the following day, towards evening.

A message had reached me at the Eastbridge Hospital early that morning, brought to me by one of Lady Mallory's servants, a circumstance which had profoundly impressed my fellow boarders.

"My lady says you're to come this evening, after supper." The man had then proceeded to give me directions, although, as he said, anyone could tell me how to get there. Tuffnel Manor was well known in the locality.

It had been another glorious day, warm even for mid-September. Only the yellowing leaves and the sudden sharp bite in the air night and morning hinted that winter would soon be upon us. Overhead, the sun still rode high in the sky, with some way yet to go before reaching the horizon. I had again done well in the market-place, and would soon have to replenish my stock. I had money in my pocket, a full stomach and was feeling pleased with myself; so pleased and contented that I wondered, as I strode along, why I was allowing myself to be embroiled once more in this affair of the Crossed Hands inn. But I knew the answer to that. God had spoken.

The knowledge didn't, of course, prevent me querying God's intentions, nor even His wisdom, from time to time; still another reason why I had felt it necessary to leave Glastonbury, and why Abbot Selwood had not tried to discourage me.

"Faith," he had told me severely, "must be absolute."

But for me, it never has been. I've always found it necessary to argue with God on occasions—even if He always wins the argument in the end.

Tuffnel Manor was surrounded by three great open fields, divided into strips by balks of sod and ploughed by the serfs and peasants who worked the holding. As I passed their huddle of cottages two men were returning home, leading a scrawny pig down from the woods where it had been turned out to forage for the day, rootling among the mast and fallen beech nuts. The Manor itself was two stories high and encircled by a moat, which I crossed by means of a drawbridge. The walls were not completely castellated, but presented narrow, shot-hole windows which overlooked the water. Inside, they enclosed a courtyard, where Bess was waiting impatiently to greet me.

"You're late," she said. "I was afraid you weren't coming, and after the trouble I took persuading my lady to see you, I should have looked a fool if you hadn't turned up." She switched her attention to the steward, who came fussing across the open space from a distant lighted doorway. "It's all right, Robert. My lady's expecting the chapman."

The man sniffed, looking down a long, aquiline nose and eyeing me with suspicion. "I wasn't told," he protested.

"My lady doesn't tell you everything," Bess answered pertly. She flashed the steward a smile, but her wiles were plainly lost on such a man.

"If you're certain, you'd better follow me. My lady's in her solar."

"I know. She has been since supper-time. And there's no need for you to accompany us. I've instructions to take the chapman to her myself."

Robert looked affronted, but, to his credit, he did not argue, merely standing aside with a shrug of his shoulders and allowing us to pass.

Bess giggled and took my hand. "He fancies himself, does that one. Fancies my lady, too; and his hopes have risen since Sir Richard's disappearance."

She led me indoors, across the great hall and up a flight of narrow, twisting stairs to Lady Mallory's solar in the upper story. In spite of the evening sunlight and the continuing warmth of the day, there was a fire burning on the hearth, and the scent of the flowers strewn among the rushes was almost overpowering. An old wolfhound, lying near the window, raised his head at my entrance and sniffed hopefully; then, realizing that I was not, after all, his master, lowered it again with an air of sorrowful resignation.

Lady Mallory also raised her head to look at me, but with a good deal more hostility than the hound. It was plain that although she had agreed to see me, she resented being indebted to anyone as lowly as a chapman.

Her face, now that I could see it properly, without the veil of two days since, was thin and discontented. Its pallor above the black gown was startling; but I suspected that it was not merely grief for her father that made it so ashen. She was a naturally bloodless creature, and in addition whitened her skin with cosmetics. Her eyebrows were plucked to a thin, single line, and the hair was shaved well back from her forehead so that not a wisp escaped from inside its cage of stiffened gauze beneath the brocaded cap. The effect was curiously masklike, but then, that was the fashion among great ladies and distinguished them from their inferiors. It was the effect that Alison Weaver had not quite managed to achieve.

I noted, too, during those long moments while I was kept shuffling my feet in the rushes, that Lady Mallory's robe was of silk, and that the ends of her girdle were tipped with gold set with rubies and sapphires. The rest of her jewelry—brooch, rings, bracelet, rosary— were all of jet as became her state of mourning, but she had been unable to resist the lure of wearing some precious stones about her person. I judged her to be a high, proud, stiff-necked woman, who put great store—more than was warranted, probably—by her tenuous royal connections, and, as a corollary, by ostentatious display of wealth and position. And no doubt her husband had been of a similar nature, hurrying up to London to offer his congratulations to a king who was more than likely unaware of his existence. Sir Richard may only have travelled with one servant for speed and convenience, but he would have left no doubt in anyone's mind that he was a man of substance. And, in his own eyes at least, a man of some importance.

I thought once again of Clement Weaver, lower in the social scale than Sir Richard Mallory, Knight, but with a father just as wealthy, and carrying a large sum of money on his person. And both men had disappeared after having contact with the Crossed Hands inn. Sir Richard had stayed there, according to Bess, and Clement had alighted from his uncle's wagon outside it. Surely it must be more than just coincidence.

"Well—" Lady Mallory's voice cut sharply across my train of thought—"sit down, for goodness' sake! You make me uneasy, standing over me like that. How tall are you?" Without waiting for a reply, she went on: "Bess! Bring a stool for your friend." There was a kind of sneering quality in the way she uttered the last word which caused the blood to sting my cheeks, but I murmured a humble word of thanks as I folded myself on to the low, three-legged stool which Bess carried over.

"It's most gracious of your ladyship to see me." One thing above all others those last few months had taught me: if you need to grovel, then do it well. People who like power and flattery don't like them in half-measures. "I very much appreciate your condescension."

Lady Mallory's icy manner began to thaw, and, for the first time since my entry to the solar, she noticed that I was not only clean, but personable as well. I don't know how old she was; certainly not young; probably all of thirty summers, but not too old to be attracted still by men. Her thin lips almost managed a smile.

"My maid tells me that you know of someone else who recently disappeared in London from the Crossed Hands inn. She has given me her garbled version of these events—" out of the corner of one eye I saw Bess pull a face—"but I should wish to hear them from your own lips. You may begin."

So I told her all I knew concerning Clement Weaver and explained how I had come by my knowledge. This necessarily entailed some personal history, and the realization that I could read and write thawed her manner even further. The fact that I had very nearly taken holy orders convinced her of my probity; a mistaken conviction, perhaps, in view of some of the priests and princes of the Church whom I have known since then, but a common enough error.

When I had finished speaking, she made no answer for a while, staring into the flames whose reflections flickered and curtsied in a wild shadow-dance across the walls. It was growing dark, and already, beyond the windows, a pale scatter of stars gleamed in the dusky heavens. A couple of young lads, fussily tailed by the steward, came in, carrying thick wax candles which they thrust into wall-sconces and lit with tapers from the glowing heart of the fire. Prompted, they closed the shutters against the encroaching night, made their obeisance to Lady Mallory and departed, again closely followed by Robert, who, before making his own deferential bow, sadly raised his eyes to the smoke-blackened ceiling. It was plain he thought himself indispensable to the smooth running of the household.

When the door had closed, and the echo of his footfalls had died away on the stairs outside, Lady Mallory removed her gaze from contemplation of the hearth and addressed herself at last to me.

"What you have just said is most disturbing. My husband stayed at the Crossed Hands inn two months since, when he went to London, as you have no doubt already learned from Bess. Yet he has stayed there in the past without ill befalling him. So why should it now? And according to your story, no connection was made between the disappearance of this . . . this . . ."

"Clement Weaver," I put in, and she nodded graciously.

"This Clement Weaver and the Crossed Hands. Indeed, if I understand you aright, the boy's father and uncle made thorough inquiries there."

"If your ladyship will forgive me, the landlord could hardly be expected to answer their questions truthfully, assuming he had something to hide. And it seems a fair assumption in the circumstances. Until hearing of your husband's disappearance from Bess, I had been strongly of the opinion that Clement Weaver had been set upon by thieves, robbed and his body disposed of in some manner. Though why footpads should bother to remove all trace of their victim did trouble me a little, I must confess . . . May I inquire what happened to Sir Richard's and his servant's horses?"

"They were still tethered in the Crossed Hands yard, the saddle-bags packed and ready for departure. My husband had settled his account earlier in the morning, shortly after rising. He had wished to be off, he said, as soon as possible after breakfast."

"And that was the last that anyone saw of him? Or said they saw of him?"

"At breakfast, yes."

"And Jacob Pender?"

"He slept in the stable and ate in the kitchen with the other servants."

"And the landlord . . . Do you know the man's name?" Lady Mallory shook her head and I continued: "The landlord swore to this?"

"Of course."

"What was the last that anyone remembers seeing of

your husband and Jacob Pender?" In my anxiety to get at the facts, I had forgotten, as I had done at the Weavers', my humble status. I received a sudden flashing look from those haughty eyes and at once set about retrieving my position. "If your ladyship will be so gracious as to tell me."

"They were seen together in the courtyard by one of the cook-maids, through the kitchen window. They were standing by the horses' heads, talking. She thought they seemed to be arguing, but could not be certain. Just then the cook called her to get water from the well and to start cleaning the vegetables for dinner. It was some while before the girl looked out again, and by that time, my husband and Jacob Pender had vanished. The horses, however, were still there, ready saddled for the journey, tethered to the bar beside the mounting-block." Lady Mallory drew a deep breath, steadying her voice. "That was the last known sighting of either of them."

"Provided you believe the girl's story," I said quietly. "Presumably it was told to your father or to one of your men?"

"Yes. When Richard failed to return home on the appointed date, I at first despatched some of my servants to inquire after him along the way. When they came back, having been as far as London without news, and having received this account from the maid at the Crossed Hands inn, my father insisted on going himself. He was very unwell, but I was unable to dissuade him. He, too, could find no trace of my husband or of Jacob Pender, and when he asked after them at the inn, the cook-maid was summoned to tell the same story."

"And did he believe her?"

This time, Lady Mallory did not seem to notice my impertinence. She lifted one hand to her face, shielding it from the heat of the fire.

"He had no reason to disbelieve her. There was nothing at all to suggest that Richard and Jacob Pender had come to harm. No bodies have ever been discovered." She raised her eyes suddenly and looked straight into mine. "They have simply disappeared, like your Clement Weaver, off the face of the earth."

CHAPTER
8

 In the quiet which followed Lady Mallory's last remark, Bess stirred uneasily on her stool in the corner, where she had retired to listen. It was as though for the first time some sense of evil or impending disaster had touched her consciousness. I suspected that until now Sir Richard's disappearance had been something of a joke to her; a cause of prurient speculation that he might have absconded with a secret light-o'-love whom he had maintained in London. Suddenly, the seriousness of the situation, the very real possibility that harm could have befallen her master, had been borne in upon Bess, and she was frightened.

Her fear seemed to transmit itself to Lady Mallory, whose fingers began closing and unclosing convulsively around the arms of her chair. Perhaps she, too, had toyed with the idea that her husband could have left her for another woman; had not been totally convinced that anything dangerous had happened to him. Bess had assured me that Sir Richard and his wife were happy together, but who knows what really goes on beneath the surface of a marriage? What one partner truly feels for another? Lady Mallory might have had good reason for thinking herself deserted. Certainly she had abandoned her efforts at search with surprising speed, but, to be fair, the death of her father must have considerably occupied her thoughts and time during the past few weeks.

The silence had grown uncomfortable. I nervously cleared my throat and said: "As I told your ladyship, I promised Alderman Weaver that on reaching London I would make what inquiries I could for his son, even though, at the time I thought it foolish. Now, however, I feel that there must be some link between both his and your husband's disappearance and the Crossed Hands inn; enough, at any rate, to justify my taking an interest in the place. If I discover anything, I will inform you."

With an effort, Lady Mallory stopped fidgeting, clasping her hands together in her lap. The firelight turned the silk of her robe from black to plum to amber.

"I should be grateful for any news of Sir Richard." She spoke stiffly, and I could see that the idea of being obligated to a common chapman did not please her. But, like Alderman Weaver, she realized that I had advantages not enjoyed by her servants nor even by the Sergeant of the Watch. No one would suspect me of over-much intelligence nor of having any interest in her husband's disappearance. I was in a position to make inquiries without actually seeming to do so, and might also pick up scraps of information which would give me a clue to his fate.

I rose from my stool and made her a bow. "That is agreed, then. And now, I must take my leave. It's dark and I have a long walk back to Canterbury."

She said reluctantly: "You must have food and drink before you go. Bess! Take your friend to Robert with instructions to feed him, then come straight back here. I want you to brush my hair before I go to bed. And you can find Matthew for me. I need him to sing to me before I sleep." Lady Mallory shivered suddenly, as though someone had walked over her grave. "I shall ride the nightmare, otherwise."

Bess came across and curtsied demurely, but it was obvious from her expression that she was disappointed by the command for her immediate return. She had had hopes, that girl, as I had, of a fond and protracted farewell. But it was not to be. With a pout of resignation, she inclined her head in my direction and said: "Come with me."

The steward's room was next to the buttery at the back of the house, and was furnished as befitted his exalted status among the household servants. A fire burned on the hearth beneath the carved stone mantelpiece, which was painted red and blue. The rushes covering the floor had obviously been fresh that morning: no stale odors arose from them, such as would have been noticeable after one or two days. A long table stood in the center of the room, and, in addition to a couple of benches, there was also a single armchair, old and blackened, it was true, but carved from good, solid oak. Tallow candles flared in the iron wall-sconces, sending shadows across the scarlet and white painted walls. A comfortable room for a steward; perhaps just a little too comfortable. I recalled Bess's words concerning Robert's aspirations. Maybe they were founded on firmer ground than she had thought. Maybe Lady Mallory had given him reason.

Robert was none too pleased to be made personally responsible for my welfare. When Bess had delivered both me and her mistress's instructions to him, he looked annoyed, giving me one of his high-bred stares, which he plainly copied from my lady.

"Surely," he protested, "this . . . this person can be seen to in the kitchen."

Bess turned on her heel with a provocative swing of her hips. "Those were my instructions. I am simply the messenger. But you would be unwise to disregard them."

She sent me a farewell glance across her shoulder, fluttered the long dark eyelashes and then was gone. Robert and I were left facing one another.

"You'd better sit down," he said at last, indicating one of the benches drawn up to the table. He went to the door, opened it and yelled a name into the drafty corridor. After a lapse of some moments, a young boy appeared, knuckling the sleep from his eyes. The steward cuffed him. "Dozing again, in front of the range? Tell Cook to prepare some food and ale for the chapman here. My lady's orders. Bring it in here when it's ready. Now, get along with you, and don't be all night about it!"

The lad was clearly glad to escape and vanished swiftly. Robert seated himself in the armchair and tried to ignore my unwanted presence. He, too, I judged to be of some thirty to thirty-five summers; a little older, possibly, than his mistress. He had sandy hair, and was not unhandsome if one overlooked a tendency to baldness. His high-bridged, aquiline nose was the strongest feature of a thin, almost cadaverous face, giving his features a misleading strength of character. But vanity sat in the pale blue eyes and gave him his dominant expression.

There was silence between us until the boy returned, bearing a mazer of ale in one hand and a loaded platter in the other, both of which he set down on the table in front of me. Then he slithered quickly from the room before there was time to incur any more of the steward's bile. I addressed myself eagerly to the food. It was some hours since I had last eaten and I had not realized just how hungry I was.

There were several slices of thick black bread, cheese and butter, wrapped in dock leaves. A small bowl containing blackberries sweetened with honey, and a slice of curd tart flavored with ginger and saffron completed the meal, which I munched my way through with relish. The cook had done me proud, considering that I was only a common chapman who could hardly expect distinguished treatment. Robert stared doggedly into the fire while I ate, but as I lifted the mazer of ale to my lips, he finally condescended to address me.

"What was your business with my lady?"

I toyed for a minute with the idea of misleading him; pretending that Lady Mallory had wanted to buy some of my wares. Then I recollected that I did not have my pack with me. I had left it in what I trusted were the safe hands of the Hospital Warden. After a few seconds more of deliberation, I decided to tell the truth. Robert would probably learn it from Bess, if not from Lady Mallory herself, eventually.

So the story was repeated yet again, from my encounter with Marjorie Dyer in Bristol through to this present evening and my meeting with his mistress. I felt sometimes as though I could tell parts of it in my sleep.

When I had finished, Robert pursed his lips and frowned. "My lady wants him found, does she?" he asked, referring to Sir Richard.

"Does that surprise you?"

He shrugged, realizing that he had either given too much away or created the wrong impression, and hastened to put matters right.

"I should have thought it obvious, after all these weeks, that Sir Richard is dead. I am merely surprised that my lady has consented to you wasting your time."

I glanced at him and saw that he spoke more in hope than from any deep conviction. Nevertheless, the assumption of his master's death was a reasonable one, unless he knew of circumstances which made it improbable. I probed gently.

"Is it possible that Sir Richard could have had a leman in London, with whom he might have wished to elope?"

The steward gave this idea short shrift, and rightly so. "Leaving everything he valued most behind him? His house, his clothes, his worldly goods! Your wits are woolgathering! What leman is worth such a sacrifice? My master could have spent as long as he wished away from home, so my lady knew of his intentions. No, no! Some ill has befallen him on the journey home. There is no other explanation."

I shook my head as I swallowed the last of my ale. "You forget. The horses were left at the Crossed Hands inn. Whatever happened to Sir Richard and his servant befell them in London, as it did to Clement Weaver."

The steward was not interested in the fate of Clement Weaver, pursuing thoughts of his own.

"Besides, Sir Richard was not a man for womanizing. I doubt if he was ever unfaithful to my lady." Nor of much use to her either, his tone seemed to imply, but I made no comment. Robert continued: "His passion was wine. He would travel miles, brave all hazards, to taste a recommended vintage. His people were vintners, two generations back, who made their fortune and married into the nobility. Not that there's lack of precedent for such a happening. Geoffrey Chaucer's father was a vintner, and Chaucer's granddaughter married the Duke of Suffolk. And the present Duke, Chaucer's great-grandson, is married to no less a personage than the present King's sister."

I noted a predatory gleam in his eye. If such things could turn out so for one family, why not for another? If his lady really were a widow, there might be hope for him yet.

I got reluctantly to my feet. The warmth of the fire was pleasant and I had no wish to leave it, but I had to be on my way. Roused from the contemplation of a rosy future, the steward turned his head, becoming once again aware of my existence.

"You're going? You'll be sleeping in a ditch tonight," he added, not without a certain satisfaction. "Curfew's past. The city gates will be shut."

I smiled maliciously. "Oh, there are ways and means

of getting into a town after dark, if you know them. Then one only has to avoid the Watch . . ." I winked conspiratorially.

His thin face assumed a prim expression. Plainly he felt that one who had so nearly embraced the religious life should be above breaking the law. He asked: "What have you decided with my lady?"

"I've promised her that I'll try to discover what has happened to her husband, and send her word if I do."

"And what do you think are your chances?"

"Of finding out the truth?" I considered the question. "More, perhaps, than I thought when I made a similar promise to Alderman Weaver to try to find out what happened to his son. Now, at least, I feel that the Crossed Hands inn may be central to the mystery. It's the place to begin my inquiries, at any rate."

The steward nodded. "And what do you think are the chances that Sir Richard might still be alive?"

There was the sharp smell of a candle as it guttered and died. The shutters were still open to the warm night air, and I could see a thin, ragged slip of moon hanging low over the distant trees. "If you want my honest opinion, none," I answered, trying to ignore the sudden flicker of relief in the pale blue eyes. "I think he and Jacob Pender and Clement Weaver are all dead, but how, and by whose hand, I have as yet no idea."

"And motive?" Robert asked. "What do you say to that?"

I hesitated, unwilling to commit myself, but with so little doubt in my own mind, I was forced to admit: "Robbery. Sir Richard was a wealthy man and Clement

Weaver was carrying a large sum of money about his person."

The steward frowned. "But surely you told me earlier that no one was aware of that fact, except his father. Not even his sister."

I was suddenly very tired and my mind felt dull and stupid. I needed to forget this problem for a while and sleep. In any case, there was nothing further I could do now until I got to London. I determined to set out as early as I could the following morning, but before that, I wanted my bed and the spiritual refreshment of solitude. I lifted my stout ash stick from the floor where I had laid it.

"I really must be on my way," I said. "I don't know the answer to this puzzle yet, and I may never do so. Maybe your mistress would do better to place her reliance in the officers of the King, as would Alderman Weaver. Nevertheless, I shall do what I can and perhaps God will crown my endeavors with success."

I held out my hand in farewell, but could see at once that I had affronted Robert's dignity. He was a steward and did not shake the hand of a lowly chapman. It dawned on him, too, that for the last half-hour he had been talking to me as though I were his equal, and he shrank back in his chair as though contaminated. I let my arm sink slowly to my side again, not bothering to disguise my contempt. He did at least get to his feet and summoned the boy to show me out, but that was to ensure that the house was properly locked and barred after my departure.

I made my way along the track, dimly discernible in the darkness, swinging my cudgel vigorously to discourage attacks from lurking footpads or other prowlers. I was glad to shake the dust of Tuffnel Manor from my feet. Apart from Bess, I had formed no favorable opinion of its inmates and thought it an unhappy household. That did not mean, however, that I would do less than my best to discover what had happened to Sir Richard and Jacob Pender.

I learned much later that had I waited another twenty-four hours in Canterbury, I should have seen King Edward and Queen Elizabeth, together with many of their courtiers, on yet another visit to St. Thomas's shrine. (With hindsight, I should guess that the King's conscience was troubling him over the necessary death of his cousin and enemy, the late King Henry.) Even so, there was much talk of the royal family among a group of pilgrims returning to London, with whom I travelled the last part of the way. And once again I heard the name of Lady Anne Neville.

The pilgrims were poor and on foot, like myself, and I had fallen in with them some six or seven miles outside the capital. I had spent a congenial morning discussing with a priest from Southwark William of Ockham's theory that faith and logic could never be reconciled, and that therefore ecclesiastical authority was the sole basis for religious belief.

"If faith and reason have nothing in common," I argued, "then God can literally move mountains. Reason tells me that it cannot be done, but William of Ockham insisted that belief is not rational. Yet that means that religion is beyond logic and not subject to the laws which govern nature. I find that difficult to accept."

"But, my son, you must believe in the miracles of Christ," my companion protested, shocked, "and in the absolute authority of Mother Church."

I grinned. "So I have often been told, Father, but somehow or other, there are always too many questions to which I can find no satisfactory answers."

A silence succeeded my words while the priest marshalled his forces to deal with this Doubting Thomas. And in the quiet, I caught snatches of a conversation in progress behind me between two women, who, I had decided in my own mind, were mother and daughter. They looked sufficiently like one another to give credence to this theory.

". . . Lady Anne Neville," the younger woman was saying, and immediately the name attracted my attention. Once more, I was back in Bristol, watching that unhappy child ride along Corn Street. "It's common gossip that the Duke of Clarence doesn't want his brother to marry her because it will mean the division of the late Earl's estates. As husband to the elder daughter, he hopes to get them all. Or as many of them as he legally can."

"A downright wicked shame," her mother answered warmly. "It wasn't my lord of Gloucester who deserted King Edward in his hour of need."

"Oh, the King intends Duke Richard to have Lady Anne, you may be sure of that. But amicably, if possible, with my lord of Clarence's and Duchess Isabel's full consent."

The girl spoke with that assurance I have frequently noticed among the very poor when talking of royal affairs. And indeed, more often than not, time and events prove them correct. I have pondered the reason for this, and have come to the conclusion that it is because their own existences are so uninteresting and drab that they live vicariously through others more glamorous than themselves. They look and watch and listen, hoarding scraps of information as some of their fellows hoard money, assessing, interpreting and making valid judgments.

"It would be a good match," the older woman agreed, "and please the people. Please themselves as well, no doubt, for they've been friends since childhood, and that's a fact. Brought up together in the North, and always intended for one another by her father . . ."

I could overhear no more. The priest was speaking again, invoking the teachings of St. Augustine in his argument and desperately trying to convince me that obedience was all. I answered randomly, letting him think that he had won our battle of words, too excited now to think of anything but that I was at last within a mile or so of London, that city whose streets were reputedly paved with gold, and which had seen the making and the breaking of so many better men than I. According to my informants who had been there, it was so much bigger, dirtier, noisier, wickeder, more beautiful, more exciting, more interesting than anywhere else in England—some people said than anywhere else in Europe—that my heart was beating almost suffocatingly in anticipation. And towards evening, with the sky trailing great ragged banners of blood-red, amethyst and flame, when the distant trees netted the final rays of the sun and seemed to catch fire from within, I saw London for the very first time, lying like a smudged thumb-mark on the horizon. Somewhere inside those walls lay the answer to the riddle of Clement Weaver's and Sir Richard Mallory's disappearance. Whether or not it would ever be solved was now up to me.

PART III

October 1471
London

CHAPTER
9

 Old age is not simply a matter of rheumatic joints, defective eyesight and impaired hearing; it's waking up one morning and realizing that there is no longer any future. That is a lesson I have learned these past few years, and something which young people find very hard to grasp. They have life, love and adventure spread before them, without any hint of their own mortality.

I was exactly the same myself, on that early October day in the year of Our Lord 1471 when I crossed London Bridge and entered the city proper for the very first time. It was, as I recall, a morning of frost and needle-sharp sunlight, all white and gold. Everywhere there was brilliance and light, from the sparkle of rimed branches and rooftops to the glitter of the rutted road and the sun-spangled glint of horses' harness. I was young, strong and ready to take on the world. The thought of any personal danger in the quest which lay in front of me never so much as entered my mind.

I had spent the night in Southwark, at the home of one of my new acquaintances. And it was thanks to him that I had acquired my first knowledge of the capital. Stretched beside him on the floor of his master's bakery, saved from the cold of the night by the warmth of the ovens, I had nevertheless found it difficult to sleep on account of the noise from the house next door. In the chill of the small hours, when my friend rose to rekindle the fires for the early baking, he discovered me wakeful. When I explained my problem, he laughed.

"I should have warned you," he said, "that the house next to this is a brothel. There are dozens of them in Southwark, all belonging to the Bishop of Winchester, so the local whores are known as Winchester geese." He also told me that I could recognize a prostitute by the striped hood she wore.

I was naïve enough in those days to be shocked by this information. Innocent that I was, I had believed until then that all churchmen, fallible human beings though they were, at least abided by the rule of chastity and assisted laymen to do the same, even if they were often unsuccessful. To find out that the See of Winchester actually owned houses of ill repute gave me a jolt from which I did not soon recover.

But now, as I approached the already lowered draw-bridge, my stomach full of a shared breakfast of porridge and small beer, my pack comfortably settled on my back, my cudgel swinging in my hand, I had no thoughts for anything but my first real sight of London. At the southern end of the bridge were three stone towers with portcullises, the outer two topped by a row of traitors' heads on spikes, each sightless, grinning mask in a different stage of decomposition.

I had no difficulty passing through the gate, but the Warden had little time to answer my request for directions. "Cross the bridge and ask again," he grunted, and indeed I could see that he was busy. I had never encountered such traffic as there is in London, nor so many people. I had been told by one of the pilgrims that it was home to some forty or fifty thousand inhabitants, but my mind refused to encompass so vast a number. Now, jostled on every side by carts and wagons and foot travellers like myself, I was overwhelmed by the noise and general air of confusion. The surface of the bridge, between the two rows of overhanging shops and houses, was badly pitted, and on at least three occasions I stumbled, twisting an ankle. But each time a neighborly hand caught my elbow and prevented me from falling. I decided that London might be overcrowded and rowdy, but the people were friendly. Long before I had reached the end of the nineteen-arch span, I was feeling more cheerful and less intimidated.

I had been advised by my host of the night to make for one of the quays east of London Bridge, where ships coming up river from the mouth of the Thames docked at the wharfside and sold goods direct to customers on shore. And after my success in Canterbury my pack was in need of replenishing. Once clear of the bridge itself, I had a better view of the river, already bustling, even at that early hour of the morning, with boats and barges of all shapes and sizes. There were swans, too, gliding gracefully through the waterborne traffic, apparently unperturbed by the movement. I could see groups of men around the piers of the bridge, fishing for the smelts and salmon, pike and tench and barbel, with which the river abounded. (I learned later that they were known as Petermen, because they used nets, like St. Peter.)

At Marlowe's Quay, an eel ship had just docked, and the housewives were already gathering with their money and baskets. A big man with a broken nose and huddled in a good wool cloak against the rawness of the morning was just going aboard, while the women stamped their feet and blew on fingers blue with cold.

"Who's he?" I asked my neighbor.

She gave me a pitying look, sensing at once that I was not a Londoner.

"That's the water-bailiff, of course. He goes through the catch and throws overboard any undersized or red eels he might discover. After that, it's his job to supervise the weighers, to make sure we get good measure." She eyed me curiously. "You waiting to buy?"

I shook my head. "I'm a chapman. I need laces and threads and silks for you women to fritter your money away on."

My companion snorted. "Small chance of that, with prices rising the way they are. Mind you, things'll get better now that Edward's on the throne again, God bless him!"

I discovered that the Londoners regarded Edward of Rouen as peculiarly their own King. Big, strong and handsome, he spent freely among them, increasing the trade and prosperity of the city. And last spring he had done the impossible, by reaching his capital from the North without the loss of a single man.

I moved on, threading my way in and out of riverside alleyways and narrow lanes whose names were as yet unknown to me. The woman had told me that I needed Galley Quay, nearest the Tower, and sure enough, when I finally got there, I found a Venetian galley unloading bales of silk and velvet, barrels of spices and sweetmeats, ironbound chests of brooches and rings. Many of the goods were too costly for hawking in the streets, but I bought a remnant of damask, enough to make a dress, and a few cheaper items of jewelry. There were also some phials of perfume and scented oil, which I added to the other wares still in my pack. It was while I was paying for my purchases that I noticed the pungent smell of rotting flesh, borne upriver from beyond the walls, and learned that it came from the decaying corpses of executed pirates, whose bodies were left until three tides had washed over them, between Wapping and St. Katherine's Wharf.

I wandered back the way I had come, still dazed by everything I saw; the great cranes along the wharfsides, busily unloading spices and oranges from Genoa or cargoes of Normandy apples and fine Caen stone. The roads were jammed with traffic, carts, drays and carriages forcing a passage between wandering pedestrians; chapmen, such as myself, itinerant friars, piemen, sailors, messenger boys. The noise was deafening; people cursing and shouting; cries of "Beef ribs! Steaming hot!" "Clean rushes!" "Good sheep's brains!" "Apples and pears! Every one ripe!" Agitators haranguing the crowds; boatmen, the roughest and toughest of all the Londoners, brawling with one another over prospective clients; the continuous jangling of the bells.

By mid-morning, my head was aching and my eyes bolting from my head. The early frost had melted, leaving the roadway wet and slippery beneath the overhanging eaves. My pack was weighing heavily on my back as I dodged the offal and garbage of the streets. My initial excitement had begun to wane, and remembering suddenly that it was St. Faith's Day, I decided to go to Mass. I had already passed so many churches that choosing one was not a problem, but I wanted particularly to see St. Paul's. Even country bumpkins like myself knew its name and reputation. A friendly shopkeeper directed me towards the Lud Gate and at the top of the hill I found it, its huge steeple thrusting into the air, crowned by a golden weathercock.

I don't know what I had expected. A holy calm, a sanctified hush, perhaps. I was certainly unprepared for what I actually discovered. By the great cross, in the north-east corner of the churchyard, instead of a priest giving godly exhortations, a man in a stained leather tunic and scuffed felt boots was holding forth, well away on some political hobby-horse of his own. The cloisters were full of people walking up and down, and it did not take me long to figure out that the bulk of them were lawyers, either touting for business or discussing cases with their clients. Inside, in the nave itself, there were more of them, together with stalls selling food and drink to the pilgrims, who, like me, had come to St. Paul's to see its many holy relics: an arm of St. Mellitus, a crystal phial of the Virgin's milk, a strand of St. Mary Magdalene's hair, and the knife Jesus used for carving when he was a boy.

There were others, but I did not wait to see them. The noise and confusion here was as bad as in the streets, and I pushed my way outside again.

As I emerged from the churchyard, I saw that people were being forced to one side by a mounted sergeant-at-arms, who was clearing a pathway for a procession of horsemen just entering through the Lud Gate. The sergeant was wearing the insignia of the White Boar, and I realized then that the young man at the head of the group of riders must be Richard, Duke of Gloucester, the King's younger brother.

"You and the lord Richard were born on the very same day," my mother used to say to me when I was small; although how she came by so exact a piece of information she would never divulge. However, I accepted that we were of an age, although that was all we had in common. In every other respect, our lives had been widely divergent. Richard of Gloucester had been Admiral of England, Ireland and Aquitaine, had levied and commanded troops for his brother throughout the entire South-West, and been the King's trusted lieutenant all by the age of eleven. In the eight years since, he had grown spiritually and politically in stature, remaining, unlike George of Clarence, totally loyal to his elder brother throughout all the vicissitudes of Edward's troubled reign. Today, he was not only Admiral but also Constable of England, Warden of the West Marches towards Scotland, Steward of the Duchy of Lancaster beyond Trent, and Great Chamberlain of the realm. He had only recently returned from the North, where he had successfully subdued the last flicker of rebellion against Edward's resumption of the crown. I was a failed monk and a humble chapman. What greater contrast could there have been?

Because of my height, I had a good view of the little procession over the heads of the other onlookers. The Duke was not at all what I had imagined him to be. I don't really know what I had expected; someone big and blond perhaps, like his brothers, who had once or twice been described to me; certainly not this slight, almost boyish figure, the serious face partially concealed by a curtain of dark, swinging hair. The hysterical adulation of the crowd, cheering wildly and throwing their greasy hats in the air, was sufficient to turn the head of a much older person, but this slim young man of just nineteen showed no signs of any self-congratulation. Rather, he seemed uncomfortable and ill-at-ease, anxious to be free of the clamor. Surly, I thought; then was immediately forced to revise my opinion as the saturnine face lifted into a smile of recognition for someone near at hand. It was like the sun coming out from behind a cloud, and although the expression was fleeting, its beauty had revealed a different man. As the cavalcade moved on and the crowd dispersed, I made a guess that the Duke of Gloucester was not happy in London.

I realized that my earlier fatigue had deepened. I was not only hungry, but feeling dirty and badly in need of a wash. I made inquiries from a messenger boy, resplendent in the gold and green uniform of his master's livery, who directed me to one of the city's public wash-houses, where, for the payment of a groat, I could immerse myself in a tub of steaming water. I was fortunate, on reaching my destination, to find that it was one of the hours reserved for men. Mixed bathing was naturally not allowed, although I learned that this was not the case everywhere in Europe. A small, heavily pock-marked man in the tub next to mine, who was vigorously scrubbing his back with a long-handled brush, asked in a throaty whisper: "You ever been to Bruges?"

I shook my head, trying to work up a lather with the coarse grey soap. "I've never been outside this country."

"I've been," the man informed me in the same quiet, rasping voice. "I was a soldier, I was, until I was wounded in a street fight. In the stomach, it was. I weren't no good fer anythink after. But I was in the Low Countries fer a while afore that." The hooded eyes sparkled reminiscently. "If you're ever in Bruges, cocky, go to the Waterhalle. Cor, what! I'll tell you! Men and women can bathe together there. Naked as the day they were born! Just s'long as the woman wears a mask and don't tell you 'er name. And all with the blessing of the Duke of Burgundy, 'imself, God love 'im! I tell you, in this country we don't know 'ow to live."

I laughed, but had no ready answer. London was as much as I could cope with at the moment, and tales of foreign countries beyond the English Channel only confused me further. When we were dry and dressed again, I invited my new friend to have dinner with me, judging by his clothes, which were even shabbier than mine, that a free meal would not come amiss. He accepted with alacrity and steered me in the direction of Fish Street, which ran north from London Bridge and where there were a couple of fine inns, the Bull and the King's Head. My companion, whose name I had discovered to be Philip Lamprey—a nickname, on account of his partiality for that particular fish—chose the former.

"Not so many of the gentry come in 'ere as go to the King's Head." He added lugubriously: "I'm not easy with the gentry. You can't trust the buggers."

But there were still a number of men in the Bull whose mode of dress and richness of apparel proclaimed them well-to-do merchants or burgesses at the very least. Low-born creatures like us were directed to a smaller room where there was straw—and none too clean, at that —on the floor instead of rushes, and where the soup was served in wooden bowls rather than tin or pewter. And the pot-boy who brought our food and ale treated us with an ill-concealed contempt. His offhand manner told us plainly that he would rather be serving the gentry.

While we ate, I heard more of Philip Lamprey's past. His wife had run away with a butcher and gone up north while he was soldiering abroad, taking their two sons with her. The rest of his family, parents and four sisters, were all dead, and his one remaining kinsman, a cousin, had died in the recent outbreak of plague. He made a living as best he could by begging, an occupation which some days rewarded him handsomely, but on others left him almost destitute. He was going through a bad patch at the moment, he told me: people were less charitable than they used to be, possibly because prices had rocketed during the late troubled times. But now that King Henry and his son were dead, Margaret of Anjou in custody, and good King Edward, the Londoners' friend, safely back on his throne again, things were bound to improve.

"And when that 'appens," he said, wiping the soup from his mouth with his sleeve, "I'll buy you a dinner. 'Ow long are you goin' t' be in London? An' where are you stayin'?"

"I was hoping to find hospitality at the Baptist's Head in Crooked Lane," I answered. "I was told to go there by a man I met in Bristol, who's a friend of the landlord."

"Oh, I know it all right." Philip Lamprey drank the rest of his ale. "Off Thames Street. Crooked Lane, that is. The Baptist's Head . . . Now, let me see . . ." He stared musingly into the depths of his empty cup and, taking the hint, I yelled for the pot-boy to bring us both more ale. "That's the place on the left-hand side as you goes towards the river. Very close to the water, it is. If I remembers aright, one lot o' windows looks out over the Thames." He scratched his sparse greying hair. Flakes of dead skin fell and settled on the shoulders of his thread-bare jacket. He picked some shreds of meat from between the stumps of his teeth. "Not a big place. Not so big as the inn higher up the street, on the corner, but it's got a name fer selling very good wines. Not fer the likes of me and you, o' course. Only fer those as can afford 'em."

The pot-boy reappeared and grudgingly refilled our wooden cups from the big stone jug that he was carrying.

"This other inn you mentioned," I said, after I had taken several gulps of my ale. "Would that be called the Crossed Hands?"

My companion nodded, wheezing and gasping, having swallowed too much far too fast. "Tha's it." He knuckled his watering eyes and blew his nose in his fingers. "Much grander place 'n the other. Shouldn't advise you to go lookin' fer a billet there."

"I have no intention of doing so," I told him drily, but my grim smile was of course wasted on Philip.

"Tha's all right then. They'd only turn you away if

you did. The landlord don't encourage our sort, by what I hear.''

"What else do you hear?" I asked; then, seeing his look of puzzlement, added impatiently: "About the Crossed Hands inn."

Philip Lamprey shrugged. "Not much. Nothink bad, at any rate. Landlord's called Martin Trollope, but I don't know nothink to 'is deprimunt." He hesitated. "We-ell . . . I did over'ear someone say once as 'ow 'e was a greedy bastard. Willin' to do anythink fer money. But then, oo wouldn't?"

My heart beat faster. This wasn't evidence, but at least it added fuel to my speculations that there was something suspicious about the Crossed Hands inn. I asked: "Is Crooked Lane far from here?"

Philip gave his throaty chuckle. "Lor' luv you, no! I'll take you there, if you like, when we've finished drinkin'."

I accepted his offer gratefully, but when we finally reached Thames Street I recognized it as one of the roads I had walked along that morning. It stretched from the Tower, through the fish markets of Billingsgate to the Bridge, and was one of the busiest streets in London, so blocked all day long with carts and drays that even the nobles and their retinues, leaving the royal apartments in the White Tower, were compelled to wait, fuming and bad-tempered, until the road was clear. The cursing and swearing which constantly assaulted the ears had to be heard to be believed.

Crooked Lane itself was off that part of Thames Street known, so Philip told me, as Petty Wales; a narrow alleyway into which little sunlight filtered because of the overhanging upper stories of the houses on either side. And there, on the right-hand corner, its sign of two crossed mailed fists creaking slightly in the breeze—not, I was relieved to note, as I had imagined it in my dream—stood the Crossed Hands inn.

CHAPTER

10

 The sign creaked slightly, as though its hinges were rusty, and close beside it I noticed the iron bracket which at night would hold a torch, lighting up the name of the inn; the light which had also illuminated the face of Clement Weaver on the last occasion his sister had seen him.

The lower half of the building was made of stone, but the upper half had a timber frame, with walls of wooden lattice work and plaster. The downstairs windows, which looked out on to Thames Street, had old-fashioned shutters, but some of those above were of horn, or covered with sheets of oiled parchment. The entrance was through an archway in Crooked Lane, and the inn was built around a central courtyard. Looking through, I could see all the midday bustle of arrivals and departures, of pot-boys and serving-maids hurrying to and from the kitchens with the dirty plates and knives used at dinner. A horse, a big grey gelding, tethered to the bar beside the mounting-block, champed impatiently at the bit, awaiting his owner.

"You ain't goin' in there?" Philip Lamprey queried in my ear.

I jumped. In my all-absorbing interest I had forgotten my companion, still dogging my footsteps, and who was now peering over my shoulder into the courtyard of the inn.

I wondered how I could shake him off. It seemed ungrateful to abandon him, but I salved my conscience by reflecting that I had bought him a meal in exchange for such information as he had been able to give me. Now, however, I needed to be on my own, with no curious stranger at my elbow. But there might be one more service he could render me.

"Do you know this Martin Trollope by sight?" I asked him.

He shook his head. "Naow! Only 'eard of 'im by repitation."

I held out my hand in a gesture of farewell too marked to be mistaken.

"I must be on my way. God be with you."

He took his dismissal in good part, clutching my extended hand in his small dry one so firmly as to leave his fingermarks momentarily imprinted on my skin.

"God be with you, too, friend," he rasped hoarsely. "If you're stayin' in London fer a while, we may meet again sometime. If you ever want t' find me, I sleeps most nights in St. Paul's churchyard. If it ain't pissin' with rain, that is. On the other 'and, if I've 'ad a good day's takings, I might be in one of the Southwark brothels." He winked. "Good sport there, jus' s'long as you don' catch the pox."

It occurred to me that this must be the reason he spent some of his meager income on bathing. The Southwark stews were probably not the most salubrious of places and he was afraid of becoming infected. Not that most people considered washing to be a remedy for anything: in fact, many held that immersing the naked body in water was positively dangerous. My mother had, however, never been of that persuasion, and had insisted on my taking regular baths from a very early age, even if it was only in one of the local streams, or standing shivering in the yard of a morning while she threw a bucket of ice-cold water over me.

"I'll remember that," I said, adding as an afterthought: "Where's your pitch for begging?"

He shrugged. "I don' 'ave a pitch. I jus' asks where and when I can. But London ain't that big. You may see me around."

"Big enough for me," I answered feelingly, and he grinned. Then, swinging smartly on his heel, some of the old military discipline showing in his step, he turned once again into Thames Street, where he was soon swallowed up by the crowd. I was left standing outside the Crossed Hands inn, not quite sure what to do next or where to begin the inquiries which I had so rashly undertaken. And I had my living to earn, as well.

The sun was high overhead, but there was still a nip in the air, and I recalled the frost of that morning. It would be sensible, perhaps, to make sure of a billet for the night by a warm fire, rather than embark immediately on any inquiries. Besides which, I had not yet made up my mind what form they should take nor how I should approach the matter. A chapman could hardly walk in and start asking questions about Sir Richard Mallory and the son of Alderman Weaver without arousing suspicion. And suspicion was the thing I most wished to avoid if I were to stand any chance of unraveling this mystery. It would be best, therefore, if I presented myself at the Baptist's Head and made myself known to Thomas Prynne as an acquaintance of Marjorie Dyer, throwing myself on his hospitality for a corner to sleep in, where I should not be in the way of his guests.

I hitched my pack higher on to my back, grasped my cudgel purposefully and turned to walk on down the street. As I did so, I happened to glance upwards, to a window on the right of the archway, which looked out over Crooked Lane. It was open slightly, and I was suddenly aware that someone, whether male or female I could not tell, was standing, a little withdrawn from the aperture, in the passageway beyond. While I watched, the figure made a forward movement, as though to open the casement wider, but as it did so a voice shouted: "Get back!" and, almost at once, the window was closed.

Alison Weaver and Philip Lamprey had both been correct in their information: the sign of the Baptist's Head could plainly be seen on the other side of the alley from the corner of Thames Street and Crooked Lane, and one side of the inn did indeed overlook the river. Crooked Lane

itself was not a long street, and, apart from the two hostelries, was walled in by tightly packed houses, whose
upper stories almost met in the middle. Today, a little
thin sunshine filtered between the overhanging eaves, but
in cheerless weather it must, I thought with a shiver, be
gloomy indeed. There was, strangely enough, no twist or
bend of any kind in the road, and I wondered how it had
come by its name. The customary mounds of refuse were
heaped outside of doorways, while the narrow channel
separating the cobbles on either side of the street was full
of rainwater and rotting food. The carcass of a dead dog
lay on somebody's doorstep. This, in London no doubt as
in other towns and cities, was a serious offense, and the
owner of the animal could be heavily fined.

The Baptist's Head was entered directly from the
street, not built, like its rival, around a courtyard. It was
far smaller than the Crossed Hands, and, because of its
location, less likely to be the recipient of passing traffic.
People who stayed there would know its reputation by
word of mouth from other, satisfied fellow travellers. Its
timber front looked clean and well painted, and the front
door, which stood open, emitted delicious smells of
cooking. Beef and dumplings, I thought, my appetite
whetted. Whatever lucky person took supper here tonight
would not go hungry. I stepped inside.

I was in a flagged passageway which ended in another doorway at the far end, also standing open to the
light and air. Yet more doors flanked me on both sides,
and a narrow twisting stair led to the upper story. I wondered where they stabled the horses. This thought was
answered a moment later by a high-pitched whinny and
the shifting of hooves from the back of the inn. I walked

the length of the passage and, sure enough, there were three stalls beneath a lean-to roof, together with piles of hay and fodder, facing me across a cobbled courtyard. Further investigation revealed that the yard was reached from Crooked Lane by an alleyway running along by the Baptist's Head on the side furthest from the river. A horse, a big red roan, occupied one of the stalls, but the other two were empty. Trade was not brisk, it seemed; not, at least, for the moment.

I went back inside, but still there was no sign of anyone. The ale-room was uninhabited, but dinner had been recently served. Dirty plates and mazers scattered around the tables testified to the fact, while the absence of left-overs confirmed my impression that the food here was good. The smell of the stew was making my mouth water, even though I had recently eaten. I returned to the passage and hollered.

"Is anyone about? Thomas Prynne! Are you there?"

There was a muffled answering shout from somewhere beneath me. Then a trapdoor in the floor of the ale-room was flung back with the resounding clatter of wood hitting stone, and a man came up the steps from the cellar.

"Sir, my apologies," he began, but stopped when he saw me. "Who are you?" He noticed my pack and waved a dismissive hand. "I'm sorry, but there are no women here just at present to be needing your gew-gaws."

He was a short, powerfully built man, with a barrel chest, well-muscled arms and thighs, a thatch of grey hair and a network of fine wrinkles raying the weatherbeaten skin. His eyes, which were of a bright cornflower blue, had a twinkle in them, and his whole person radiated a contentment with life in general, and his own existence in particular, which was very reassuring. This, I thought, was a happy man.

"Thomas Prynne?" I queried, although I was sure of his answer.

"Yes. But I've already explained—"

"I'm not here to sell you anything," I cut in quickly. "A friend of yours, Marjorie Dyer, told me to look you up if I was ever in London."

"Marjorie Dyer? Of Bristol?"

"The same. Also Alderman Weaver mentioned that you might be persuaded to give me a corner to sleep in for the time that I'm here."

"Alfred Weaver?" he demanded incredulously. The eyes twinkled more than ever. "He said that? Now what in heaven's name would one of our leading Bristol Aldermen be doing talking to a chapman?" The West Country accent was still very strong.

I grinned. It was obvious that Thomas Prynne had the measure of his old boyhood friend.

"It's a long story," I replied. "Not one to be told in a moment. Later, perhaps, when you have more time. I'm off to the Cheap presently to sell my goods, if I'm lucky. But I'd like to be sure of a night's lodging first. I can pay my way if the accommodation is not too fancy."

Thomas Prynne shrugged. "Any friend of Marjorie's can have a bed here for nothing, and welcome. We have only one visitor at present. Another is expected later this evening, but that leaves a room empty. It's yours until we need it. Then, if you're still here, you may sleep in the kitchen for as long as you like." He smiled, the lines deepening around the corners of his eyes. "But I shall expect you to take your food and ale here."

"Judging from the smells coming from your kitchen, that won't be any hardship," I answered cheerfully. "But Marjorie Dyer and I have only a passing acquaintance. I shouldn't wish to take advantage of your generosity without making that plain."

Thomas regarded me steadily. "You know, you've aroused my interest. Why should such a brief encounter have caused her to mention my name?" He indicated one of the barrels ranged around the walls. "I have an excellent ale which I don't hand out to everyone. Surely, you can delay your visit to the Cheap long enough to sample it with me and satisfy my curiosity at the same time. There are still sufficient hours of daylight left for you to sell at least some of your goods."

I hesitated, feeling that I had already wasted enough precious hours that day, but in view of his most kind offer of free lodgings, what choice did I have but to comply?

I moved to one of the long wooden tables near the old-fashioned, central hearthstone and sat down. I noticed how beautifully clean everything was, the table-tops scrubbed, the sawdust and scattered rushes on the floor freshly laid.

"I'll answer any questions you want to ask," I said.

When I was a child, on winter nights, when the door of our cottage was shut against the darkness outside and there was little else to do but sleep, my mother would sing to me. One of the songs I remember best was of the sort where you keep repeating the words you have sung before, but adding a little extra information each time. I reflected that my story was getting like this, growing in length with each retelling, so that now, it took me almost half an hour before I reached my arrival in London. Fortunately, Thomas Prynne was an excellent listener, giving me his full attention and not interrupting with unnecessary questions or exclamations of wonder and astonishment. When I had finished, however, he did permit himself a long, low whistle.

"A very strange story. You intend to keep your promise to Alfred Weaver, then?"

I twisted my cup of ale between my fingers. "I have to confess that I had all but forgotten it by the time I got to Canterbury. If the truth be told, I thought the Alderman's idea that I might be of some assistance extremely foolish. I thought—I suppose I still do think it possible—that Clement Weaver fell a prey to footpads." I could see by Thomas Prynne's vigorous nod of the head that this was his own opinion. "But what happened in Canterbury made me less certain. It also seemed that God meant me to take a hand."

My companion looked dubious. "There is such a thing as coincidence, a more frequent occurrence than you might at first imagine." He added: "Young Clement's disappearance was a terrible thing, but robbery and death are not uncommon in London."

I frowned, watching him pour more ale into my empty cup. "The point is, we don't know for certain that Clement's dead. And that is what bothers me. Why would footpads take the time and trouble to remove the body?"

Thomas Prynne grimaced. "A difficulty, on the face

of it, I grant you. But there might be reasons. Perhaps, with winter coming on, they were desperate for clothes. Perhaps they were disturbed, or thought they might be disturbed, before they could safely strip the body, so they carried it away. Not as much of a problem as it seems, if there was more than one of them. And these fellows often work in gangs."

The need for clothing was something I had not previously thought of. But even so, if the robbers had money, they could buy clothes. And there was still the disappearance of Sir Richard Mallory to be considered. I shook my head.

"I'm convinced," I said, "that there's some mystery about the Crossed Hands inn. Do you know anything of Martin Trollope?"

"I know him by sight, naturally, and to give the time of day to. Other than that, we have little contact. We are, after all, rivals for custom in the same street." Thomas smiled ruefully. "And all the advantages are on his side. Location, size, royal patronage and connections . . ."

"Tenuous ones, if my information is correct." What was it Bess had said? "Trollope is merely the cousin of a dependant of the Duke of Clarence."

Thomas laughed outright at that. "It's easy to tell, Roger Chapman, that you haven't long been in London. Such a 'mere' connection is not to be sneezed at. A great deal of trade at the Crossed Hands is by recommendation from the Duke himself. I wish I could boast as much in the way of royal support." He sipped his ale, regarding me thoughtfully over the rim of his cup. "So! What do you intend doing by way of fulfilling your promise to Alfred Weaver?"

"I don't know yet," I admitted. "I haven't as yet decided on a plan of action. But something may occur to me."

"I'm sure it will," Thomas assured me drily. "You seem a very resourceful and competent young man. A chapman who can read and write! Well, well! Wonders will never cease. I can read a little, myself, but putting pen to paper is a skill I have never mastered. I have to rely for that on my partner, Abel Sampson." I must have looked surprised, because he laughed. "Did you think that I run this place single-handed?"

"No. No, of course not. I just hadn't thought about it at all, I suppose. As I've already told you, Marjorie Dyer and I had only the briefest of acquaintances. You're not married?"

Thomas shook his head. "I've never felt the need. My experience is that wives are generally a hindrance. There are plenty of women for the having in any city, but especially in London. I learned to cook when I was land-lord of the Running Man, and with only three bedrooms, not all of which are occupied at any one time, the de-mands on me are not excessive. Abel and I are our own cellarers, servers and chamberers. That way, with no other wages to pay, and no dependants, we manage to make a living. It's not easy, but at least the place belongs to us, whereas in Bristol the Running Man was the prop-erty of St. Augustine's Abbey, and all my efforts simply resulted in the Church getting richer, with no reward to myself."

"You deserve to do well," I said, adding fervently:

"This ale is the best I've ever tasted and, as I remarked before, the cooking smells delicious."

"You shall sample it tonight, when you return from the Cheap." He rose to his feet, picking up our empty cups. "As for our ales, and especially our wines, Abel and I do the buying ourselves. The ships from Bordeaux tie up west of the Steelyard, at Three Cranes Wharf. It means early rising to be ahead of the vintners, but we don't begrudge that extra effort. In time, we hope to gain a reputation for selling the best wines of any inn in London."

I was beginning to admire this man more and more. He was plainly determined, against the odds, to make a success of his venture; and he had all the Bristolian's canniness with money which should enable him to succeed. He also had humanity and a vein of humor which I found attractive, and I wished him well.

"When I return this evening," I said, "I should like to talk to you about the night Clement Weaver disappeared. If you can spare the time, that is."

He smiled down at me. "We're expecting another guest, as I told you, but he's been on the road from Northampton for the past few days, and according to the carrier who brought his message, doesn't anticipate being here until late. So, if the opportunity arises . . ." He broke off with a shrug. "Our other guest, by the way, you'll meet at supper. An impoverished gentleman who is rapidly becoming poorer yet on account of all the litigation he's involved in. He's come to London for the second time this year to petition the King. Something to do with land and a contested will." He sighed, as if for the folly of the human race. "London is full of people like

him, pouring their money into the pockets of the lawyers.''

I nodded. I remembered seeing them earlier that day
in St. Paul's cloisters.

A step sounded in the passage outside, and a moment later, a tall, thin man appeared in the open doorway
of the ale-room. Thomas Prynne nodded towards him.

"This is my partner, Abel Sampson."

CHAPTER
11

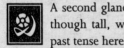 A second glance showed me that Abel Sampson, though tall, was not so tall as I was. (I use the past tense here because, with the passage of time, I have become a little stooped. Arthritic limbs have inevitably taken their toll.) He was, nevertheless, a considerable height, standing well over five-and-a-half feet, the top of his head reaching to the level of my eyebrows. It was his slender frame which made him appear taller than he really was. I don't say he was emaciated, but he was certainly extremely thin, and the contrast he made with Thomas Prynne was almost ludicrous. I had to school my features rigorously to prevent them breaking into a grin.

Abel Sampson was also a great deal younger than I had expected; not much above twenty-four or -five summers I guessed. He had sandy hair and eyebrows, pale blue eyes and bloodless, almost invisible lips which looked as though they did not know how to smile. Humorless, I decided. And here again, as so often in the past, my first impressions were wrong. In those days, as I have said somewhere before in this tale, I was not a good judge of character. I jumped too far and too fast to false conclusions. Abel Sampson suddenly smiled, and, like Richard of Gloucester, whom I had seen earlier that same day, his face seemed to light up from within, turning him into a different person.

"Is this the man we've been expecting?" he asked his partner.

Thomas shook his head. "No, no! I'm sure I told you that Master Farmer would not be arriving until late this evening." He spoke severely, obviously deploring this lapse of memory.

Abel looked sheepish. "So you did," he agreed. He added, addressing me: "I have a terrible memory."

I laughed, getting to my feet and picking up my pack. "Then I'm in good company," I replied, "because I have, too." I turned to Thomas Prynne. "I'll be off, now. I can't afford to waste any more daylight. But I'll be back for my supper. I hope to have made some money by then, so make it a large one."

"You shall have as much stew as you can eat," he promised. "In the kitchen with us, or in here with our guest, Master Parsons."

Before I could open my mouth, Abel had made the decision for me.

"Eat with us," he advised, grinning. "The lugubrious Gilbert will be very poor company after yet another day wasted in the law courts."

I hoisted my pack on to my shoulders. "Precisely what I was intending to suggest myself." I moved towards the door of the ale-room. "Besides, there's something I want to discuss with Master Prynne here."

"Call us Thomas and Abel," that worthy reproved me. "We're on Christian name terms with any friend of Marjorie Dyer."

Abel Sampson agreed wholeheartedly. "And we'll call you Roger." He nodded at my pack. "I wish you luck with your selling."

I thanked him and asked directions to the Cheap. Moments later, I was once again walking up Crooked Lane in the direction of Thames Street. Outside the Crossed Hands inn I paused for the second time that day, staring thoughtfully up at the window which had been shut so roughly earlier in the morning. I had seen a figure hovering behind it, I was sure. Someone must have been there to have provoked so angry a reaction from the second person, the one who had closed the casement. I tried to recall the voice I had heard shouting "Get back!" and the more I thought about it, the more I was convinced it was a man's.

I suppose I stood there longer than I realized, because all at once someone said angrily in my ear: "Get a move on, chapman! I don't want your sort loitering here."

I swung round to find myself confronting a man of very nearly my own height, and a great deal broader. In fact, he was of quite considerable girth. He had a thick, bushy beard which concealed most of his face and was of the same dark brown as his curly hair. His eyes, too, were brown, and also what could be seen of his skin, which was weather-beaten to the color of a walnut. Burly was the word which came to mind. If he had not been so well dressed, in a fine linen shirt beneath a soft woolen tunic, with boots of good quality leather on his feet, I should have taken him for a rough ex-soldier. There was something military in his stance and the way he barked out his orders. But his use of the first person and his tone of authority made me fairly certain that this was Martin Trollope.

"I'm sorry," I said, swallowing my anger and speaking as humbly as I could. "But this is my first visit to London and I find everything fascinating. I was admiring your windows."

"Why?" was the brusque retort. "You've seen windows before, haven't you? Now, get away from here! I told you, I don't want your sort hanging around."

The man was definitely on edge, and I felt that it was time to make him still edgier.

"Are you the landlord, Martin Trollope?" I asked.

He glowered fiercely, but I noticed his right hand playing nervously with the buckle of his red leather belt.

"And if I am, what's it to you?"

"Nothing. Nothing," I answered placatingly. "It's only that I've heard of you. I was in Canterbury last month and was fortunate enough to have sold some of my wares to Lady Mallory of Tuffnel Manor." It was a lie, but only a white one. "Her maid told me afterwards about Sir Richard's disappearance from this inn. And also that of his man, Jacob Pender."

Martin Trollope's reaction was not quite what I had

hoped for. "Oh, him!" he grunted sourly. "Left still owing me money. Hadn't paid for his own or his servant's lodging." I forbore to say that this was not Lady Mallory's story, and he continued: "And his father-in-law, Sir Gregory Bullivant, God rot him, refused to settle the account. Said I had no proof that Sir Richard had absconded without paying."

"But surely," I argued, "Sir Richard must have intended to return. He left the horses."

"Which Sir Gregory took away," was the vicious retort. "A pox on him!"

"He's dead," I answered shortly.

Martin Trollope eyed me narrowly. "You seem to know a lot about it."

"Lady Mallory's maid was very loquacious."

"'Loquacious,' is it?" he sneered. "That's a big word for a common chapman."

I thought it time to go. I had no wish to arouse his suspicions until I had gathered a good deal more information than I had at present. And I couldn't conceal from myself that I found his attitude somewhat disappointing. He had not started guiltily on hearing me pronounce Sir Richard Mallory's name; on the other hand, he did strike me as a man who was hiding something. I couldn't say exactly what it was that made me feel this way, except for his general air of uneasiness and his dislike of strangers hanging around the inn. A chapman could not be an unusual sight, and it was not what I *was* that had attracted his attention. No; I was convinced it was the fact that I had been staring up at that particular window, and with such concentrated attention, which had brought Martin Trollope hotfoot outside to move me on.

"I'll be going, then," I said, and took a few steps towards the corner of the street before turning to glance once again at the casement just above our heads.

This time his reaction was far more rewarding. "Get away!" he commanded furiously; and I knew then that Martin Trollope's had been the voice which had shouted "Get back!" that morning.

"God be with you," I answered magnanimously and turned, well satisfied, into Thames Street.

As I pushed my way along that crowded thoroughfare, however, I was conscious that something was nagging at the corners of my mind; some little fact which was troubling me and making me uneasy. But the more I tried to pin it down, the more elusive it became, dodging in and out of other thoughts which obscured it. By the time I had been sworn at by three passers-by for not looking where I was going, I knew I should have to let it go, at least for now, and trust that the puzzle would resolve itself presently. And I had work to do. I set out resolutely for the Cheap.

West Cheap, or Cheapside, is also known simply as The Street, because it's so famous. I don't suppose there's a soul in the whole of England, then as now, who hasn't heard of it. It's not what it was when I was young, but as I've remarked before, that goes without saying. My children and grandchildren will feel the same when they're my age. But when I first saw it, in that October of 1471, I thought it must be the most magical place in the whole wide world.

Cheap, of course, comes from the old Saxon word

"chipping," meaning a market: there was nothing cheap, in its current usage, about The Street. There were shops stuffed with silks and carpets, tapestries brought from Arras, gold and silver cups and plates, the most magnificent jewelry. My eyes were dazzled and I felt like a child in fairyland, in spite of the fact that it is heresy to believe in the little people. (But then, for someone who still half acknowledges the existence of Robin Goodfellow and Hodekin and the terrible Green Man, how can I not believe in the world of fairies?) A conduit—the Great Conduit, I heard it called—brought fresh spring water all the way from Paddington, still smelling of herbs from the village meadows. There were grocers' and apothecaries' shops; and I saw grey Bristol soap being sold at a penny the pound, less than half the price of the hard white Castilian. The ordinary black liquid soap was only a half-penny.

There was the Standard, originally made of wood, now being rebuilt in stone, where Lord Say had been murdered by the followers of Jack Cade twenty-one years previously; the church of St. Mary-le-Bow with its famous bell, so called because it was raised on arches; the great cross erected by King Edward the first, presently being rebuilt at a cost of well over a thousand pounds through the generosity of the capital's citizens. There was the Mercers' Hall situated along the north side, and the beautifully painted and decorated houses of the merchants. There was . . . But I could go on boring you forever with the wonders of that part of London. All I can say is that since that day, I have met many people, including foreigners, who speak with awe of Cheapside, its wares and its treasures.

I thought I should be unable to sell much there, and was thinking of moving on, when I had my first customer. After that, it was easy. I had never before sold as much in a couple of hours as I did that afternoon. I realized after a while that people came to the Cheap to buy and were therefore in a spending mood. They didn't much care who they bought from, provided they could afford what was on offer. And my wares were undoubtedly cheaper than those on display in the shops. I attracted the poorer citizens by the dozens.

Mind you, I don't say that my appearance didn't have something to do with it. A lot of my customers were women; and if that sounds boastful, I'm sorry, but it happens to be the truth. I've always believed in using the gifts God gave you, and trading on my good looks to gain an advantage over my competitors never worried me or made me feel ashamed. I flirted with the younger women and flattered the older ones—another proof, if you need any more, that I was unsuited for a life of self-abnegation.

When the church bells began tolling for Vespers, I packed my remaining wares into my pack and prepared to walk back to Crooked Lane, thinking hungrily of my supper. The fragrance of Thomas Prynne's delicious stew lingered in my nostrils, making my mouth water in anticipation, and I set off for the Baptist's Head with a swinging stride and a light heart, remembering the good business I had done that afternoon. It was still chilly, and remnants of the morning's frost hung about the streets like grimy cobwebs. But storm clouds were gathering. It would not be so cold that night and might even rain.

London continued to bewilder me, and although I knew I must be moving in the right direction, I nevertheless managed to lose my way. I suddenly found myself facing a huge and forbidding stone building, which seemed to my inexperienced eyes to be a fortress of some description. There were three massive arched gates fronting on to the street, and two of them were locked. At the third, carts were drawn up, loading or unloading goods, and I realized suddenly that this must be the Steelyard, home of those Hanseatic merchants who were the descendants of German traders established by the Saxon kings in Dowgate. I knew of their reputation from Marjorie Dyer, who had told me all about them that evening in Bristol; how the Easterlings lived a celibate life, with no women allowed inside the Steelyard walls; how they had their own two Aldermen to represent them in the city government; how they stayed aloof from other Londoners; how they held a monopoly of the Baltic trade. In the event of an attack upon the capital, they were responsible for the defense of Bishopsgate, and consequently kept, or so the story went, a suit of armor in every room.

It was while I was staring—gawking, my mother would have called it—at this imposing edifice, like a true rustic unused to such sights, that I found my eyes focused on one of the carters, who, with an assistant, was unloading great bales of cloth. There was something familiar about the man's face, but I could not immediately recall where I had seen him before. Then, as though becoming aware of my scrutiny, he turned his head in my direction, and I recognized him as the carter employed by Alderman Weaver for the transport of his cloth to London. I went over, waiting patiently by the horse's head until he should be free to speak.

This took some while as there were at least half a dozen bales of the unbleached cloth to be unloaded; and when that task was finally accomplished, the man followed the Germans into the Steelyard and was gone for some time. When he emerged at last, he was ripe for someone to complain to.

"Every single bloody bale weighed and examined," he grumbled. "The Easterlings, they don't trust no one."

"They pay well, though," I said, remembering my conversation with Marjorie Dyer on Marsh Street quay.

The carter sniffed. "Don't make no difference to me, son. I don't see none of it. They pay my employer, or his bailiff, when 'e comes up to London. And I get paid last of all."

"I'm sure Alderman Weaver doesn't keep you waiting any longer than he has to."

The man looked at me sharply. "What do you know of the Alderman?" he asked. He cocked his head on one side, his eyes bright with curiosity. "I've seen you some place before. Are you from Bristol?"

"I've been there," I admitted. "I was born in Wells." He nodded, as much as to say that my accent gave me away. "And you're right, we have met before, if only briefly. I was with Marjorie Dyer one morning last spring when she spoke to you. The wharf at the end of Marsh Street."

"Oh yes," he said, but it was obvious that although he remembered my face, he had no recollection of the occasion.

"She gave you a letter to deliver to her cousin," I reminded him, but the carter merely shrugged.

"She often does that. So do a lot of other people.

You'd be surprised what I get entrusted with. Good job I'm honest."

I agreed. "There's been no news, I suppose, since then, of Clement Weaver?"

He stared at me as though I'd taken leave of my senses and quietened his restless horse.

"No! And never will be!" he answered scornfully. "He's dead and gone, and it's only the Alderman, poor sod, who won't accept it." He eyed me shrewdly. "Told you all about it, did she? Marjorie Dyer." When I made no reply, he went on: "She'd like the matter cleared up, I dare say, just to get back the Alderman's attention. Oh yes!" He winked broadly. "She has hopes in that direction, does Marjorie. The second Mistress Weaver, that's what she wants to be. She always was ambitious. Never took kindly to being the poor relation, waitin' on the rest of 'em. And now the daughter's married and gone to live in Burnett, it's possible Marjorie might have brought the Alderman up to scratch by this time, if he'd been able to think about anyone else except his precious Clement."

I wasn't altogether surprised by this revelation, confirming as it did what I already knew about the relationship between the Alderman and his housekeeper. So Alison had married the foppish William Burnett and gone to live with him in his home village, had she? That, too, was unsurprising, even if it were to be regretted. A high-spirited girl like that deserved someone better.

The carter mounted the box and took the reins between his hands. He still had deliveries to make and plainly wanted to be finished by nightfall. I stood away from the horse's head to let him go, but he hesitated a moment longer.

"Whereabouts in the city are you lodging?" he asked me.

"The Baptist's Head in Crooked Lane." I interpreted his look as one of astonishment. He had not expected me to be staying at an inn, but rather at a religious hostelry, where accommodation was free and the diet of black bread, salt bacon or fish, and water. He also looked resentful, and I hastened to reassure him that I was not that much richer than he. "I traded on my brief acquaintance with Marjorie Dyer and the Alderman, I'm afraid. Master Prynne has most kindly agreed that I can sleep in the kitchen." I thought it prudent to make no mention of the bed I had been offered.

The carter nodded, accepting my explanation. Indeed, he even seemed pleased by it. He dropped the reins and fumbled in the leather pouch fastened to his belt.

"I remember Thomas Prynne," he said. "Landlord of the Running Man in Bristol before he came to London to make his fortune. Wanted to do as well as his old friend, Alderman Weaver, if you ask me. A bit of envy, I should guess, although that's not a bad thing if you want to get on in this world. Myself, I'm content to be what I am and follow the calling God gave me. My wife, she says that's just an excuse for laziness, but I've learned to ignore her nagging. In my experience it's the only way to get the better of women. You've just got to pretend they're not there."

I laughed, remembering my mother. "They won't stay ignored, that's the trouble."

He seemed, at last, to have found what he was looking for and triumphantly produced a folded paper from his pouch. "Here," he said, holding it out to me. "What a piece of luck you're going to Crooked Lane. It'll save me an extra journey. This letter's from Marjorie Dyer to her cousin, Matilda Ford, who's cook at the Crossed Hands inn. P'raps you'd be kind enough to deliver it for me.'' As I took it from him, he gathered up the reins again and thanked me. "God be with you," he said, giving his horse the office to start.

I stared stupidly after him as he vanished up the street, the slow clop of the animal's hooves dwindling into the distance.

CHAPTER

12

 My mind was reeling. Marjorie Dyer had a cousin who was cook at the Crossed Hands inn! I just stood there blindly in the middle of the street, trying to make sense of this information.

Marjorie was also distantly related to Alderman Weaver, but whether through her mother or her father I had no idea. Whichever it was, this Matilda Ford was a cousin on the other side of her family; an obvious enough deduction, as the Alderman had plainly known of no connection with the Crossed Hands inn which he might have exploited at the time of his son's disappearance. And Marjorie had not enlightened him. Why not? There was only one conclusion to draw, however reluctant I might be to do so. Marjorie Dyer was in league with the robbers.

No, no! The idea was preposterous! But why was it? What, after all, did I know about her, except what she herself had told me? And I had been a witness to the way Alison treated her, half-friend, half-servant; the very attitude to stoke the fires of Marjorie's resentment. Furthermore, if she really had plans to become the second Mistress Weaver, Clement's removal would be to her advantage. With him gone and Alison provided for by marriage to a wealthy husband, why should the Alderman not make a will leaving everything to Marjorie? Things began to make sense.

Another thought hit me like a bolt of lightning. I had seen for myself that Marjorie slept in the Alderman's bed, so what more likely than that he confided in her from time to time? He had probably told her that Clement would be carrying a large sum of money on that particular visit to London, so all she had to do was notify her cousin in advance, sending a letter by the carter, and afterwards claim to be ignorant of the fact . . .

And yet . . . And yet . . . There were still pieces of the puzzle which did not fit. Marjorie could not possibly have foreseen the circumstances which would have deposited Clement outside the Crossed Hands inn, alone, on a dark and stormy evening. By rights, he should have parted from his sister at Paddington village and ridden on to the Baptist's Head with Ned Stoner. My brain felt addled, but one fact stood out clearly, and I glanced down at the letter I was holding. At least, I now had a reason for entering the Crossed Hands inn, which not even Martin Trollope himself could quarrel with.

A hand descended heavily on my shoulder and a guttural voice spoke angrily in my ear.

"Vy don't you move? You are obstructing the vaggons."

I turned to find one of the Easterlings glaring at me, and I also became aware that several of the carters were shouting abuse. I was blocking the traffic. I mumbled hasty apologies and made my way back to Thames Street, resolving on no more short cuts. I was not yet familiar enough with the London streets to attempt them, so I kept straight on until I came to the corner of Crooked Lane and the Crossed Hands inn. My eyes raised themselves instinctively to that window to the right of the courtyard entrance, but it was firmly closed and there was no sign of life behind it. No shadow, however faint, was silhouetted against the oiled parchment. Silence reigned.

Stifling a feeling of disappointment, I hitched up my pack and turned under the archway, clutching Marjorie Dyer's letter like a talisman.

It wasn't difficult to locate the kitchens on the north side of the courtyard; all the shutters stood wide open and there was a great clatter of pots and pans, as well as a strong smell of cooking; not the single, delicious aroma that emanated from the kitchen of the Baptist's Head, but a mixture of scents; roasting meat, rising bread, simmering broth, together with stale fish and a whiff of garlic. It failed to whet my appetite, and I thought with contentment of the fragrant meal awaiting me a few yards further down the street.

There were plenty of people in the courtyard, stabling horses for the night, drawing water from the well, carrying food up the outside stairs to one of the bedchambers, but, by great good fortune, no sign of Martin Trollope. I walked over to the kitchen door and stepped inside.

For a while no one took any notice of me; indeed, I doubt if they were even aware of my presence, until the scullion, a pale-faced boy with a constant sniff, looked up from pounding some pinecones in a mortar and asked in a nasal whine: "Wotch you doin' 'ere? Wotch you want? The landlord don't allow no peddlers."

His words attracted the attention of others, and a fat woman with flour up to her elbows shouted: "Get off with you! Go on! Get out! Lad's right. Master Trollope don't allow no peddlin'. This is a respectable inn, this is."

"I'm not selling," I answered with a virtuous air of injured innocence. I waved the letter. "This is for the cook, Matilda Ford, from her cousin in Bristol."

There was a moment's silence while all heads turned in the direction of a table at the far end of the room, where a woman and two girls were preparing vegetables and skinning rabbits. The woman stared suspiciously at me for a second, then, wiping her hands on her apron, came slowly towards me.

"Who are you?" she demanded. "And why have you brought my letter? Marjorie usually sends it by the carter."

She was tall for a woman, but small-boned, with wisps of foxy-colored hair escaping from beneath her cap; not at all how I would have expected a kinswoman of Marjorie's to look. And yet she reminded me of someone. Was it Alison Weaver, now Lady Burnett? Perhaps I was wrong in my assumption that Matilda Ford was not related to the Weavers, but belonged to the other side of Marjorie's family.

I explained my involvement as briefly as I could, but was met with nothing except a scowl as one thin hand shot out and grabbed the paper.

"That fool of a carter had no business entrusting my letter to a stranger," she snapped. "All right! You've given it to me. Now get on about your business." Before I had time to protest at such uncivil treatment, her head jerked round to address the girls behind her. "And what are you great gormless lumps sniggering at? Get on with your work this instant! You know we're shorthanded since Nell was dismissed. Do you hear me?"

The girls looked sulky. One, who plainly had more courage than the other, demanded truculently: "Well then, if we're short 'anded, why don't that new girl come down and pull 'er weight. Pretendin' she's ill all the time an' stayin' upstairs! She ain't no more ill than I am. An' the master lettin' 'er get away wiv it! It ain't fair!"

"You mind your own business, my girl," Matilda Ford retorted sourly, "or you'll find yourself turned off. If Master Trollope says she's to be left alone until she's better, that's nothing to do with you." She added, muttering under her breath: "Though why he lets himself be taken in by such a baggage—" She broke off abruptly, recollecting my presence. "Are you still here? What are you waiting for? You've given me the letter, so get on about your own affairs." She went back to the table, picked up a wicked-looking knife and started on another rabbit. The girls, more sullen than ever, continued chopping vegetables.

Everyone else ignored me, so I had no excuse to prolong my stay. But I was intrigued by this kitchen-maid who was exempt from duty, even though they were shorthanded in the kitchens. Such concern for the health of his cook-maids somehow did not fit the Martin Trollope I had met that morning. Something smelled, and it was not just the fish which was being gutted by the scullion. I walked thoughtfully out into the cooler air of the courtyard, glancing about me. A big pile of logs was stacked against a wall outside the kitchen door and, loosening the straps of my pack, I slipped it from my shoulders. The shadow cast by the logs hid it from all but the most inquisitive eyes. Then I strolled across the yard, unnoticed in all the bustle of a new arrival, and mounted the outside stair to the balcony. Three doors opened off this into what I presumed were the main guest-bedchambers, but facing me at the far end was a fourth door, leading, I hoped, to the inn's private quarters. I sent a quick, furtive glance down into the courtyard, found I was still unobserved, and with a few swift steps and a lift of the latch was in a narrow corridor, a continuation of the balcony, but now walled in, with a door to my left and a window to my right, the latter covered in thick oiled parchment. Furtively, I opened the casement and peered outside. I was looking down into Crooked Lane where it joined Thames Street, and, glancing to my right, I could see the entrance to the courtyard. This, undoubtedly, was the window which had attracted my attention early that morning, and I speculated who the person was who had been standing here. My guess— and I felt almost certain that it was correct—was that it was the missing cook-maid.

Kitchen servants were never allowed above stairs, their place of work also being their sleeping quarters. It was as strange, therefore, as it was intriguing that one of their number should not only be permitted to plead illness, but, even allowing that her sickness might be genuine, be cosseted in seclusion until she was better. And particularly by Martin Trollope. And if the girl were his mistress, which was highly unlikely, why would he wish to conceal her? It was as though her presence at the inn was a secret. Yet not completely: Matilda Ford and her two assistants, at least, were aware of the young woman's existence. They regarded her as having come to the Crossed Hands inn to work and were angry at what they saw as her shirking. But where did the girl fit in with Clement Weaver's and Sir Richard Mallory's disappearance? That was something which I had yet to fathom.

I opened the door on the left-hand side of the corridor and peeped inside, but to my bitter disappointment there was no one in the room. The room itself was small and scantily furnished; a truckle bed, neatly made up with clean, lavender-scented linen, a joint stool beside the fireless hearth, and a chest, probably containing clothes, were the only items in there. The thing which immediately drew my eyes, however, was a piece of embroidery flung down on the bed, as though it had only recently been abandoned. I picked it up carefully and examined it, wondering, as I did so, at the delicacy of the design; at the fragile, muted tones shading from gold to palest green, from egg-shell blue to white. This was an example of the famous Opus Anglicanum, learned by every woman of birth and standing, and eagerly sought after by the rest of Europe. These lovely patterns and exquisite colors were prized even among the treasures of the Papal Court. And here again, of course, I write from knowledge acquired much later in my life: at the time, I only knew that this had to be the handiwork of a gentlewoman. The rough, chapped hands of a peasant woman, like my mother, could never have made such tiny, fragile stitches.

As I stood staring at my find, I was aware of a sudden flurry of movement on the periphery of my vision. The next instant, a hand grabbed my shoulder.

"You again!" It was Martin Trollope, his face livid with anger. "What in the name of Satan are you doing sneaking about my inn, prying into things which don't concern you?" He dealt me a swinging blow, and, big though I am, he almost knocked me off my feet. "I've a good mind to call the Watch!"

I don't know what made me take a chance. My brain felt addled by the buffet to my head, and my ears were singing as though a whole aviary of birds was inside them. But I managed to retain my balance and said, with as much dignity as I could muster: "Go on, then! Call them."

Trollope's eyes narrowed and he looked as if he might hit me a second time. But all he said, through lips stiff with rage, was: "Get out! Now, before I change my mind. And consider yourself bloody lucky!"

"You're not going to call the Watch, then?" I asked, as insolently as I dared.

"I've told you! *Get out!*" He spoke through clenched teeth and his right hand was bunched into an enormous fist.

I'm not a coward; being the size I am, I've never had need to be. But he was a very big man, and there seemed

KATE SEDLEY • 154

little to be gained by picking a quarrel with him on his own territory. He had only to shout to bring half a dozen of the inn's servants running to his aid, and I should be thrown ignominiously into the street, probably acquiring a black eye or a cut lip in the process. It was far better that I went quietly while I could. Nevertheless, it was interesting how reluctant he was to call the Watch.

I replaced the embroidery on the bed and Martin Trollope became aware of it for the first time. His eyes bulged and his face, or what was visible of it above his beard, turned a dull, bloated red, giving the game away completely. This was not the work of some woman guest who was staying at the inn, or he would have been indifferent to its discovery. This had been done by the mysterious kitchen-maid, who so obviously was not one.

I raised my eyes and smiled into his, letting him know that I was conscious of this fact and had realized its implications. He gave a snort of stifled rage and thrust his face forward on its short bull-neck, pushing it so close to mine that our noses were almost touching.

"You breathe a single word of my affairs outside this inn and you'll be sorry your mother ever bore you! That's a promise, and don't think for one moment that I can't keep it."

I was not so foolish. I had no doubt that a character like Martin Trollope had sufficiently powerful connections both among the nobility and the criminal fraternity of the city to make it good. It was something I might have to risk in future, but not just at present. With a sense of relief at being able to postpone the evil day, I edged past him towards the door. Two minutes later I was again standing in the courtyard, humping my pack on to my back, Martin Trollope glaring balefully at me from the balcony. There was no chance for me to return to the kitchen for another word, however brief, with Matilda Ford, and I had to content myself with a defiant wave at the landlord as I passed under the archway and emerged once more into Crooked Lane, turning my feet in the direction of the Baptist's Head.

It was now well past the hour of Vespers. The brilliance of the morning with its sparkle of frost had faded to a uniform greyness as daylight waned. A thin layer of cloud, stretched like muslin, obscured the sun; the houses appeared flat and two-dimensional as though cut from paper against the darkening sky; the bustle of Thames Street was no more than the roaring of some distant ocean on a remote and foreign shore, the sound muted by the overhanging houses.

As I covered the yards between the Crossed Hands and the Baptist's Head, I wondered whether to reveal what I now knew about Marjorie Dyer to Thomas Prynne, or to keep my own counsel. What, after all, did I know for certain? Not enough to make accusations. And yet, I felt that I would be glad of his opinion on what appeared to me to be her very suspicious conduct. But then again, he might be incapable, or at least reluctant, to pass judgment on a friend. It was a dilemma I had still not resolved by the time I reached the inn. I decided to wait and see what happened; to see how he responded to a hint on my part that Marjorie might not be as innocent as she seemed.

The smell of the stew was even more delicious, as

though some delicate herb or spice had been added since my departure. I sniffed appreciatively as Thomas met me just inside the doorway.

"Sorrel," he said, laughing. "I always add a little to my soups and stews. How did your day go? Did you make any money?"

I grinned and jangled the coins in my pouch. "Enough to buy me the best supper you have, breakfast in the morning and pay for my night's lodging, as well. Tomorrow, I hope to do even better."

He threw up a hand in protest. "I've told you, any friend of Marjorie Dyer's sleeps here free." He jerked his head towards the door at the far end of the passage. "The well's in the yard, near the stable."

I thanked him, left my pack and stick inside the ale-room and made my way outside. I drew up a bucket of ice-cold water, bathed my face and hands, shook off the surplus drops and let my skin dry in the chill evening air. The red roan shifted restlessly in its stall, kicking with its back hooves against the flimsy door. I guessed that it belonged to Gilbert Parsons, the hapless litigant mentioned by Thomas and Abel.

By the time I returned indoors, Gilbert had put in an appearance; a painfully thin man with the melancholy expression of a bloodhound. He was seated in the ale-room, eating his supper, which, as well as the stew, consisted of bread and cheese, a dish of rampion—the root boiled and served in a thick white sauce—a dish of orache, also boiled, and to follow, a sillabub decorated with sugared almonds. Just the sight and smell of it all made my mouth water, and I hoped fervently that we would be eating as well in the kitchen.

We did, washing everything down with a fine Bordeaux wine, the like of which I had never tasted before and rarely have since. Thomas Prynne had not exaggerated when he said that he and his partner bought only the best to put in their cellar. Even my untutored palate could appreciate its velvety texture and contrast it with the rough red wine we novices had occasionally been given to drink at the abbey. I'm afraid I made a pig of myself that mealtime, gorging until I could eat and drink no more.

"I'm glad he's able to pay for his food," Abel remarked to Thomas, "or we might have found ourselves sadly out of pocket."

Thomas nodded in agreement. "You're a good trencherman," he said, addressing me. "Mind you, you've a big frame to keep going. It's natural you should be a hearty eater."

I smiled at him. Or at least I tried to smile, but my lips refused to obey me. The heat of the kitchen, the enormous meal, but above all, the wine to which I was unaccustomed, had all combined to make me stupid and sleepy. I gave a prodigious yawn and stretched my arms until the bones cracked. I should have liked to go to bed, but it was not yet dark and curfew had still not sounded.

"Come and sit by the fire," Thomas Prynne suggested, indicating what I presumed to be his own chair, as it had arms. "You can sleep off the effects of your supper while we prepare for Master Farmer from Northampton. He must be here soon if he wants to avoid putting up for the night outside the city. The gates will shut within the hour. Abel, be a good fellow and look outside to see if he's coming."

I watched Abel leave the kitchen through a sleep-drugged haze, sinking into the chair and stretching my legs out before me. My eyelids were already closing. In half an hour or so, I promised myself, I would go into the yard to get some air. But for the present, replete, I was content to let food and wine and the heat of the fire do their work. I drifted over the borderline of sleep.

CHAPTER
13

 Suddenly I was wide awake, jerked into awareness by the sound of my own snoring. For a moment or two I was completely lost, unable to make out where I was or remember the earlier events of the evening. Then memory came crowding back, and I realized that I was no longer seated in the chair before the kitchen fire, but stretched full length on a bed, where, presumably, Thomas and Abel had carried me. I must have slept deeply and dreamlessly for several hours, the landlord and his partner finding it impossible to rouse me when it was finally time to retire for the night, so they had been forced to hump me upstairs between them. I sat up cautiously and peered around, my eyes slowly growing accustomed to the dark.

I felt dreadful. My head thumped and pounded as though my brain were trying to burst through my skull. The inside of my mouth was dry as tinder and tasted appalling. My limbs were as limp and as useless as those of a sawdust-stuffed doll, while my head swam every time I tried to focus my eyes. Hurriedly I closed them again and slumped back on the bed.

I swallowed the bile which rose in my throat and waited patiently for the nausea to subside. I had at least learned a valuable lesson: I had no head for wine. After what seemed like an hour but was probably no more than a quarter, I began to feel a little better; enough, at any rate, to sit up again and ease my feet to the floor. Moonlight rimmed the shutters, inlaying them with a faint mother-of-pearl radiance, and I made myself stand up, tottering slightly, then go across and set them wide. The storm clouds of early evening had vanished, torn to rags by a rising wind. They slid by, unveiling the stars, and somewhere close at hand the breeze took hold of a loose shutter, rattling it on its hinges. I peered out into the darkness, but could see nothing. I was staring down at the yard at the back of the inn, and all was still and silent. Even Gilbert Parsons's horse was sleeping.

I closed the shutters and turned back once more into the room, my eyes now able to see quite plainly. Apart from the narrow bed on which I had been lying, there was nothing except an oak chest supporting a tallow candle in its holder and a tinder-box. This, obviously, was the chamber kept for passing strangers when the other two rooms were full, or for people without much money, who, like me, were simply glad of bed for the night and not too fussy. The rushes on the floor smelled musty, as though they had not been changed for a couple of days.

I was suddenly conscious that my bladder was over-full, a result of all the wine I had drunk at supper. Many people, then as now, would not have hesitated to urinate in a corner, but I have always had a fastidious streak, inherited from my mother, which others are inclined to jeer at. I know my fellow novices at Glastonbury thought it hilarious when I insisted on going outside to piss, even in the depths of winter. They used to pass all sorts of obscene remarks, but I never minded, because I was big enough to accept that kind of teasing with good humor. I suppose physical height and strength do tend to make one placid.

I struck the steel against the flint and lit the candle from the burning tinder. Then, shutting the box and re-placing it on the chest, I quietly opened the door of my room and stepped into the darkened corridor. As silently as I could, so as not to disturb the other inmates, I crept down the stairs and made my way along the passage to the door at the back of the inn. I reached up to the great iron bolt at the top, only to discover that it was already withdrawn from its socket. Glancing down, I saw that the one at the bottom had not been shot home either. And when I tried the key, I found that that, too, was unturned. Surely Thomas Prynne and Abel Sampson were not the kind of men to be so careless. I felt a sudden frisson of fear, as though something evil was lurking on the other side of the door, waiting to grab me.

I noticed my hand was shaking, the wavering can-dleflame sending shadows flickering drunkenly over the walls, and I pulled myself together. Everyone was careless now and again, I told myself severely; even the best of us had moments of forgetfulness and did stupid things. Resolutely I lifted the latch and stepped outside, into the moon-washed courtyard. In the distance I could hear the tolling of a bell and realized what had really roused me from my drunken stupor. Not my snoring, but the old habit of waking at two hours past midnight for the office of Matins and Lauds. It was too strong even for the potency of Thomas Prynnes's good wine.

The wind immediately snuffed out my candle, so I put the holder down on the floor inside the door, and tiptoed across the courtyard to the privy, which cast a thick black wedge of shadow in the moonlight. As I relieved myself, I heard the gentle snicker of a horse as it blew softly down its nostrils. Then there came an answering whinny from the stall at the end of the stable. Two horses? Of course! While I had been dead to the world, Master Farmer, the other guest, had arrived. I smiled ruefully to myself. What must my hosts think of me, so green and so unable to hold my liquor?

The chill night air had cleared my head wonderfully, and my limbs had ceased their palsied trembling. My stomach, too, had decided to behave, after one or two squeamish moments. I returned to the inn, carefully locking and bolting the back door after me. As I passed the ale-room, I could see where the last embers of the fire winked and glowed on the now almost empty hearth. I mounted the stairs to the landing, and my ears were at once assailed by the stertorous snoring of another guest, who had also drunk too deeply. I felt a little cheered to know that I was not the only drunkard. But there was no sound from behind the third guest-chamber door, the one furthest from mine. There all was silent as the grave.

An unexpected wave of nausea made my stomach heave, and left me once again urgently in need of fresh air. There was a window at the end of the landing and I hurriedly pushed it open, inhaling the smells of the nearby Thames. This window was at the front of the inn, and by turning my head to the left I could see the river as it flowed past the wharf at the end of the street, its surface washed first silver and then gold by the moonlight. Slowly the sickness receded and I began to feel better. I looked to my right, in the direction of the Crossed Hands inn, expecting Crooked Lane to be empty at this hour of the morning. And at first glance it appeared to be so. Then, suddenly, I was aware of a figure enveloped in a thick hooded cloak moving swiftly and silently up the street, hugging the shadows cast by the houses opposite. Whether it was a man or a woman was hard to tell at that distance because the cloak reached to the ankles and the hood was up, drawn tightly about the head. As I watched, my whole body rigid with anticipation, my fingers stiffly clutching the sill, the figure drew level with the Crossed Hands inn and vanished through the archway. At almost the same moment Thomas Prynne's voice said behind me: "By Christ, Roger Chapman, you gave me a fright! What are you doing up and about at this time of night?"

He was wearing a voluminous white night-shift, which made him look like a friendly ghost, and a nightcap pulled well down over his ears. In one hand he held a lighted candle.

"I'm s-sorry," I stammered. "I didn't mean to wake you."

He looked me up and down, smiling quizzically.

"It's something, I suppose, that you can stand on your feet. The state you were in, I didn't expect you to come round until morning. You must have extraordinary powers of recovery."

"I'm not used to wine," I apologized. "I had no idea it would affect me so badly." I remembered something. "And we didn't have our talk about Clement Weaver."

"Oh, that!" He shrugged and shivered a little as the wind blew in through the open casement. "A waste of time, if you want my opinion. Shut that window, there's a good lad." He frowned. "What's it doing open?"

"I needed some air," I explained. "I wasn't feeling so well."

Comprehension dawned in his eyes and he chuckled quietly. "Well, I can't say I'm surprised. Better get back to your bed now."

As he turned away, I said: "I had to go downstairs, to the yard. You'd left the back door unlocked and unbolted."

He shook his head. "Nonsense! You must be mistaken. I locked and bolted it myself. I always see to it personally before I come upstairs at night. With so many thieves about, I won't risk leaving it to Abel. Young men are inclined to be careless."

"The door was open," I insisted. "I went into the yard to relieve myself, and it was unbolted."

Thomas frowned again. "You're absolutely certain?

You didn't imagine it? Wine fumes can be extremely potent and sometimes confuse the brain."

"No, I'm sure," I answered. "I'd been awake some while and was perfectly sober. But just now, through that window, I saw someone walking up the street to the Crossed Hands inn."

"At this hour?" He sounded incredulous and, pushing past me, threw wide the casement again.

"Whoever it was has gone now," I told him. "He—or she—went into the inn."

Thomas withdrew his head, once more closing and fastening the window. "Why do you say 'she?' Did you think that it might have been a woman?"

"It was impossible to tell. The person was wearing a long cloak with a hood."

He gestured dismissively. "A late reveler, perhaps. A lot of respectable citizens break curfew and manage to avoid the Watch. It's not difficult. I've done it myself."

"I'm sure this wasn't a reveler. There's something suspicious about that place."

Thomas smiled indulgently. "So you said before, but you haven't really convinced me yet." He shivered again. "We'll talk about this in the morning, if you want to, but for now, let's get back to bed. I have to be up before cockcrow. I need my sleep."

"I'm sorry," I said again. "Forgive me. I shouldn't have kept you."

"Do you feel all right now?"

I nodded. "I gather Master Farmer arrived safely. I heard his horse in the stable, when I was outside in the yard."

Thomas took a deep breath, looking puzzled. "I

don't know what's been going on here tonight, or if it's all in your head, but there's no horse but Master Parsons's in the stable. Master Farmer failed to arrive before curfew. He must be putting up for the night outside the city walls. We shan't be seeing him now until tomorrow.''

I went back to bed but could not sleep, lying wide awake in the darkness. The throbbing in my head was now a dull ache, but I was no longer feeling sick. My stomach at last seemed able to cope with its burden.

Had I been wrong in thinking that I had heard a second horse? At the time I was sure that there were two in the stable, but I might have been mistaken. I had been shut inside the privy and had certainly not been at my brightest. Yet I could have sworn that one whinny had answered another. I got up and went over to the window, opening the shutters . . .

". . . horse. He says he heard it.'' It was Thomas Prynne's voice, floating up to me from the yard below. I could just make out the faint glimmer of his candle.

"I thought he was out cold until morning.'' It was Abel Sampson speaking this time. "Perhaps we'd better look round and make sure all's well.''

Obviously, Thomas had been more disturbed by what I had told him than he let on, and had roused his partner to accompany him on a search of the inn and its premises. I closed the shutters softly and lay down again, first divesting myself of my shoes and tunic. The back door had definitely been open: I had not dreamed it. So, if Thomas was right and he had locked it, who could have drawn back the bolts, and why? And who was the person

I had seen from the landing window, hurrying so furtively up the street and entering the Crossed Hands inn?
Martin Trollope? The mysterious cook-maid? Matilda
Ford? And who had he, or she, come to see at the Baptist's Head? What, after all, did I know of Gilbert Parsons . . . ?

My head was swimming, but pleasantly this time. I
was by the Stour once more, making love to Bess. When I
looked up, Alison Weaver and William Burnett were
standing further along the bank, watching us. Alison said:
"Leave Marjorie Dyer alone," and I saw that Bess had
turned into the housekeeper. Alison smiled at the young
man by her side, who was no longer her husband. She
slid an arm about his neck. "This is my brother, Clement . . ."

I woke to find the shutters of my room now rimmed
with a faded, rain-washed light. When I opened them, a
chill wind hit me as it raced across the sky, blowing the
clouds into an ever-changing vista of shapes. A spatter of
raindrops touched my face, and the daylight which
filtered between the neighboring rooftops was murky and
unwholesome. The weather had worsened during the latter part of the night. I shook myself free of the rags of
sleep and the last, lingering echoes of my dream, put on
my shoes and tunic, and made my way downstairs. The
smell of frying bacon greeted me from the kitchen, and
the fact that it made my mouth water and set my stomach
rumbling proved that I was completely cured. The indis-
position of the night had left me.

When I looked round the kitchen door I saw
Thomas Prynne holding a skillet over the kitchen fire, in
which he was cooking thick slabs of fat, salt bacon. On

the table were a number of wooden bowls filled with oatmeal, liberally sprinkled with saffron, two big jugs of ale and a loaf of bread, half of it cut into slices. He turned his head at the sound of my footsteps and smiled.

"Are you feeling better this morning?"

"Well enough to do more than justice to your breakfast," I answered. "I'm just going to wash in the yard. By the way, did you and Abel discover anything after I'd gone back to bed?" In reply to his questioning glance I went on: "I heard you talking under my window. I couldn't really hear what you were saying, only a few words, but I gathered you were looking around."

Thomas speared a slice of bacon with his knife and deftly turned it over. The fat spluttered and sizzled in the pan. "No, nothing," he said, "but I can explain the unlocked door. Our other guest, Master Parsons, had earlier had the same call of nature as yourself, and had carelessly forgotten to bolt it after him. He confessed as much when I took him his mazer of ale at first light this morning."

"And the other horse?" I queried, beginning to feel remarkably foolish.

"A figment of your imagination, I'm afraid. There was only Master Parsons's Jessamy in the stable." Thomas's smile deepened. "It's as I said. Wine fumes can play strange tricks."

Abel Sampson came into the kitchen, yawning and stretching his arms above his head. "God's Teeth, I'm tired. I always am when my rest's disturbed."

I felt guilty and edged towards the door. "I'll be back in a few minutes," I said, "when I've washed."

It was quiet in the courtyard, except for an occasional flurry of wind and the steady patter of the rain on the cobbles. Since childhood, I have always loved the early morning, the sense of calm before the hurrying hours gather themselves together into the urgency of midday, slide towards the boredom of late afternoon, then surge, rejuvenated, into the bustle of evening. It's a time for quiet and reflection, with a whole new day stretching ahead of me; an undiscovered territory; a promise as yet unfulfilled. I raised a bucket of ice-cold water from the well and bathed my face and hands. No doubt Master Parsons was wallowing in a hot tub in front of the fire in his bedchamber, but then, he was paying for his room. I returned to the kitchen and my breakfast.

While I swallowed my oatmeal and bacon, I discussed the night's events—or non-events, as they had turned out to be—with Thomas and Abel.

"I'm sorry," I said, "to have disturbed you for no reason."

"No harm done," Thomas answered thickly, through a mouthful of bread and honey. "And if the yard door had been left open all night, we could have been robbed. It wouldn't have taken a good thief long to discover the trapdoor and stairs to the cellar." He swallowed his food and asked: "What are your plans? Do you intend returning here again this evening?"

I nodded. "I'm stopping in London for a while yet. I haven't begun to get to the bottom of Clement Weaver's disappearance."

I saw the two men exchange glances before Abel said: "There isn't any mystery, you know, except for what's in the Alderman's imagination."

I accepted another slice of bacon and set about it heartily. "What about Sir Richard Mallory?" I asked him.

Abel shrugged. "This is an evil city. We hear of robberies and murders every day of our lives, don't we, Thomas?"

The landlord raised his eyebrows in agreement. "And in the late unsettled times, things have naturally been worse. To my way of thinking, both Clement and this Sir Richard were set upon and killed, and their bodies disposed of in the river. I'm sorry if I sound hard, because Alfred Weaver is a friend of mine and I've known both the children since they were little. I was as upset as anyone by Clement's disappearance and the distress that it caused his family. But I don't allow sentiment to cloud my common sense. I don't believe, as his father does, that he might still be alive somewhere, or, as you seem to do, that his death has something to do with Martin Trollope and the Crossed Hands inn. It was dark and stormy, black as the grave, the night he was due here and never arrived. The sort of night when every criminal in the city is up and about his evil business. I wasn't worried when Clement didn't show up. I thought he must have changed his mind and gone to his uncle's instead, along with young Alison. It wasn't until Ned Stoner rode in just after curfew that I realized that anything was wrong."

"What did you do?" I asked him.

Thomas shrugged and looked at Abel, who obligingly continued for him.

"We—all three of us—set out to search for him, of course. But there was nothing much we could do that night. It was too dark and wet, as Tom's already mentioned. As soon as it was daylight, we searched again and alerted the Watch. Ned Stoner rode out to Farringdon Ward to discover if by some chance Master Weaver was there, but none of us had much hope of the outcome. Neither Tom nor I had any doubts by that time that the boy was dead, especially when we learned what sum of money he had had about him.''

"That was much later, of course,'' Thomas said, beginning to gather up the dirty dishes. "After the Alderman's arrival. And now, we all have work to do, so let's get on and do it.'' He paused beside my stool and laid a gentle hand on my shoulder. "Leave it, lad, that's my advice. Don't waste your time hanging around in London. There's a whole world out there just waiting for Roger Chapman's wares. However hard it may sound, Clement Weaver and Richard Mallory are dead. Forget them.''

CHAPTER
14

 But I had no intention of forgetting either Clement Weaver or Sir Richard Mallory. I did not say so to Thomas Prynne, however. There was something in both his and his partner's manner which indicated clearly that they did not wish to be troubled with the matter. And why should they? I asked myself, as I left the kitchen and crossed the passage to the ale-room in order to collect my pack and stick. They were convinced, as I had been earlier, that the two men had been set upon by thieves, robbed and murdered and their bodies disposed of in the river. They were busy people, and had no time for less credible theories. Furthermore, I had not told them of Marjorie Dyer's duplicity. But, then again, was it duplicity? It was not a crime for her to have a cousin who worked at the Crossed Hands inn. It was simply that she had apparently not mentioned the fact to the Alderman . . .

Gilbert Parsons was in the ale-room, eating his breakfast, his lean, sad face wearing the same abstracted expression. He turned his soulful, watery blue eyes towards me and said in a hollow voice: "Nuncupative wills are the Devil's handiwork, and lawyers the Devil's instruments. Never trust them, and never pin your faith in litigation."

"I don't intend to do so," I answered cheerfully, then paused, frowning. "You haven't seen my pack and stick here anywhere, have you?"

It was Thomas who answered my question, as he came bustling along the passage to see if his guest wanted more ale.

"They're in your chamber. We took them up, out of our way, after we'd carried you to bed last night." He gave his deep throaty chuckle. "You mean you didn't notice them? You must still have some of that wine clogging your brain, my lad!"

I thanked him, looking suitably sheepish, and mounted the stairs once again. The doors of all the bed-chambers now stood open, revealing the interiors of the rooms. My natural curiosity was immediately aroused and I looked inside the other two, noting appreciatively the difference in furnishing. The largest of the three chambers, the one which should have been occupied by Master Farmer from Northampton, contained a huge four-poster bed, hung with a tester and curtains of rubbed, but nonetheless good, red velvet. Beside it was a small oak cupboard, on top of which still reposed a jug of ale and a loaf of bread; the "all-night," placed there the previous evening for the guest who had failed to arrive. In addition, there was a wax candle in a pewter holder, and a tinderbox. A fine oak chest was ranged against one wall and had been opened in readiness to accommodate the traveller's clothes and perfumed with lavender and spices. A mirror of polished metal hung above it, and, in the farthest corner from the bed, stood a night-commode. The rushes scattered on the floor were redolent with the scent of dried flowers. A pile of logs lay ready to be lit on the hearth. A room, indeed, for the privileged guest.

The chamber next to it was Master Parsons's. A smaller bed with tester and curtains of unbleached linen was still unmade, the sheets crumpled and tumbled, and a deep hollow down the center of the goose-feather mattress. The candle beside the bed was only of tallow, and the clothes-chest, like the commode, was made of elm wood. The rushes on the floor had lost their perfume and were plainly two or three days old. Which brought me to my own room, with nothing but a truckle bed and the battered oak chest, one of its hinges broken and the other missing. Smiling ruefully, I looked about me for my pack and stick.

They had been placed in a corner of the room which was always in shadow, and explained why I had previously overlooked them. I was relieved to know that I was not still suffering from the effects of last night's wine. I humped the one on to my back and grasped the other, only to find myself unexpectedly wishing that the stout ash plant was a slender willow wand, that magical staff which protects travellers from harm. I shook my head vigorously to clear it of such nonsensical thoughts. What danger could I possibly be in?

Downstairs, Gilbert Parsons was getting ready to set out for the law courts, while Abel was busy removing dirty dishes from the table. Thomas was nowhere to be seen, but the trapdoor to the cellar had been heaved back against the floor, revealing a flight of worn stone steps. I nodded at Abel and handed him the money for last night's supper. "I'll be back again this evening," I said.

He grunted. "You may have to sleep in the kitchen if we've managed to rent out your room." He obviously deplored Thomas's open-handedness.

"Of course!" I smiled disarmingly. "Master Prynne has already made that plain."

Then, whistling, I turned and walked out into the street.

At the top of the lane I paused, staring into the courtyard of the Crossed Hands inn. I wondered if I could chance my luck and get inside, without encountering Martin Trollope. But just at that moment he appeared on the balcony, shouting down to one of the ostlers who was leading a horse out of the stables. I badly wanted to speak to Matilda Ford again, but decided that the time was not propitious.

I had decided, over breakfast, that this morning I would sell my wares in the Farringdon Ward, going from house to house, knocking on doors. That way, I hoped to locate the Alderman's brother, John Weaver, and learn anything he could tell me. Consequently, I made my way along Cheapside and out through the New Gate to the noisy, stinking cattlemarket of Smithfield, where, on great occasions, tournaments and jousting were held. Beyond, lay St. Bartholomew's Priory, famous for its annual fair, the numerous Inns of Chancery and the long string of shops and houses strung out along the River Fleet.

It was more than half way through the morning before, quite by chance, I knocked on John Weaver's door. As I put the question I had posed at every house so far— "Can you tell me where John Weaver of Bristol lives?—" the sallow-faced girl who had appeared in the doorway asked pertly: "And why would that be any concern of yours?"

"I have a message," I answered, "from his brother, the Alderman." And when she still hesitated, I added: "Of Broad Street, in Bristol."

"Wait here," she snapped. "I'll fetch Dame Alice."

Dame Alice was a stout, pleasant-faced woman, who wheezed distressingly whenever she was flustered, as she appeared to be now. Her faded blue eyes were wide with suspicion, wisps of hair escaping from beneath her white linen cap.

"Are you the chapman?" she asked unnecessarily, eyeing my pack. "My daughter-in-law says you have a message for my husband."

"Is he at home?" I inquired politely.

She shook her head. "He's over at Portsoken with George and Edmund." These, presumably, were the two sons whom Alison had mentioned. "The weavers need constant supervision, you know. You can't just leave them to their own devices. A lazy, idling, good-for-nothing set of people." She spoke without rancor, simply endorsing her menfolk's opinions, as was seemly in a woman. "He won't be home until just before curfew, but you can go over there and find him, if you like."

I had no desire to leave the lucrative market of Farringdon Without before I had knocked on as many doors as possible. Already, my pack was greatly depleted: I should need another visit to Galley Wharf tomorrow morning.

"Perhaps I could leave the message with you?" I hazarded. "It's to do with your nephew's disappearance."

"Clement? Oh dear, oh dear! That poor boy! Maybe . . . Maybe you'd better come in."

She led me through to the garden at the back of the house, which ran down to the river. The rain had cleared by now, giving way to hazy sunshine and a sky which stretched milk-white above the tree-tops, threaded with faint ribbons of gold. Mistress Weaver and her daughter-in-law, whom she addressed as Bridget, had been picking herbs from the little herb-garden in the shade of one wall. Cumin, fennel and others were heaped in a shallow basket, ready to be dried and stored for the winter.

Mistress Weaver folded her hands together nervously over her apron.

"What . . . what did my brother-in-law have to say about poor Clement?"

I told her as quickly as I could about my meeting with Marjorie Dyer and my talk with the Alderman, leaving out my subsequent adventures. When I had finished, it was Bridget Weaver who spoke first. Her manner had lost its initial hostility.

"Poor Uncle Alfred," she said quietly. "He can't accept what's happened. But there's nothing more we can tell you than you seem to know already. Alison, her maid

and the four men—our two, Rob Short and Ned Stoner—
arrived here late in the afternoon, not long before curfew.
But as soon as Ned had seen Alison safely inside the
house, he rode back again to the Baptist's Head. He was
only just in time as it was, before the gates were closed
for the night. It wasn't until next morning that we knew
Clement was missing.''

Her mother-in-law nodded. "My husband and sons
set out for the city immediately and spent the next few
days searching every place they could think of where
Clement might have gone of his own free will. Not that
they, or any of us, had much hope of finding him. We
sent one of our men post-haste to Bristol and the Alderman was here within a week, but by then, we knew the
worst.'' Mistress Weaver sighed. "I realize that it's difficult for Alfred to accept the truth, particularly without a
body to convince him. But, believe me, he's wasting your
time, as well as raising his own hopes falsely. My husband
and sons would tell you exactly the same if they were
here.''

It was the same story as I had heard before, with
always the same conclusion. There was no doubt in anyone's mind that Clement Weaver had been murdered by
footpads. In any mind but mine, that is. I still felt there
was a mystery to be unraveled. But there seemed nothing
more to be gleaned from either Mistress Weaver or her
daughter-in-law, so I said I must be on my way.

"You must have some refreshment before you go,''
the older woman insisted, and led the way to the kitchen.
"Bridget, my dear, fetch the chapman some ale.''

But when it came, it was sallop, a "poor man's ale,''
made from wild arum. Bridget Weaver was not such a

fool as to waste the real thing on a peddler. The two women drank an infusion of calamint, which my mother had been fond of, swearing by it as a cure for coughs and the ague. They did not offer me a seat, and I stood towering above them, as they sat at the kitchen table. Neither of them offered to buy anything from me.

I was still drinking my sallop when a swarthy, thick-set young man entered the kitchen. He bore more than a passing resemblance to Alderman Weaver, so I had no difficulty in placing him as one of the nephews. And as he stooped and gave Bridget a smacking kiss, I guessed him to be her husband. My presence, of course, entailed further explanations, which to my relief were given by Dame Alice. I felt that if I had had to repeat my story again, I should have gone mad.

When she had finished, the young man, whose name I had learned was George, grunted and pulled down the corners of his mouth.

"Uncle Alfred's a fool," he said, not mincing matters. "Clement's dead. If he wasn't, we should have heard by now." He turned to his mother. "Father and Edmund sent me to tell you that they won't be home for their dinner. There's trouble among the weavers over at Portsoken. They want more money. They say the cost of bread is rising. They're talking of sending a deputation to the King, to remind him that he promised to control the price of food this coming winter."

I remembered what the Canon of Bridlington had written in the previous century: it had been a favorite quotation of our Novice Master at Glastonbury. "*Any attempt to control prices is contrary to reason. Fecundity and dearth are in the power of God alone, so it follows that the fruitfulness of the soil, and* not the ordinances of men, will determine the cost of our goods." I had always felt that this was a little unfair, making God responsible for our problems.

Bridget said: "They're always making trouble. They want a good whipping. Is there any news from the city?"

George shrugged his big shoulders. "Only the same gossip that's been rife for the past few weeks. The Duke of Gloucester wants to marry Anne Neville and the Duke of Clarence says he shan't. And the King tries to keep the peace between them."

"Heaven alone knows why." Mistress Weaver threw up her hands. "He owes the Duke of Clarence nothing."

These were much the same sentiments as I had heard expressed by my pilgrim friends two days earlier. Interest in the King and his family seemed a popular pastime here in London.

I put my empty mazer down on the table and said quietly: "Thank you. I must take my leave now."

Mistress Weaver and the other two, who had been momentarily diverted, suddenly recollected my presence.

Bridget said: "I'm sorry we were not of more help."

I smiled regretfully, but I had not really expected to gain any further information from them. The truth of the matter lay where it had always lain, at the Crossed Hands inn. I was still convinced that that was where I should discover the truth about Clement Weaver. And about Sir Richard Mallory and his servant, Jacob Pender.

By dinner-time my pack was almost empty and I retraced my steps to the city and East Cheap, where the butchers and cookshops plied their trade. There were also fishmongers selling baked as well as fresh cod and mackerel, salmon and trout, and I wandered happily among all this abundance of fare, wondering what to buy first. In some of the shops the owners stood in the entrance, darting out to pluck me and other passers-by by the sleeve, urging us to sample what was on offer. On one occasion I saw a small man lifted bodily off his feet and carried forcefully across to a pie-stall. His little legs, in their parti-colored hose and long leather boots, kicked unavailingly against his captor.

I strolled across and tapped the pieman on the shoulder. "Release him," I said quietly, but at the same time clenching one of my hands into a fist.

The pieman hesitated while he looked me up and down. My size, however, evidently decided him. Reluctantly, and with a muttered oath, he set the man on his feet again and moved away, casting around him for his next victim.

The little man smoothed down his tunic, trying to appear dignified, but only succeeding in looking extremely ruffled.

"Thank you, my good man," he said. "I am much obliged to you."

"My pleasure," I answered. I noticed for the first time that his tunic was embroidered with the crest of the White Boar and the motto "*Loyauté me lie*—Loyalty binds me." Memory stirred. Those, surely, were the crest and motto of the Duke of Gloucester.

"May I offer you a cup of ale at the Greyhound?" he went on, indicating one of East Cheap's many hostelries.

"If you'll allow me to buy some pasties to go with it." My stomach was rumbling so hard I was sure he must have heard it.

He gave no indication of having done so, however,

merely inclining his head with a kingly gesture and waiting patiently until I had made my purchase. I had always heard that the nobles' servants were often grander than their masters, which accounted for so many of them being nicknamed "King" or "Prince" or "Bishop." I followed him into the ale-room of the Greyhound, and was amused to notice that, once the ale was ordered, he tucked me away in a corner, where we should be unnoticed. He had no wish to be seen by his cronies and fellow servants in the company of a chapman. Only gratitude had prompted his gesture.

I ate my pasties, one of which he fastidiously declined, unperturbed by his obvious embarrassment. Conversation was difficult at first, but after a while the ale began to loosen his tongue. By the time we had both drunk our second cup he was becoming, if not garrulous, then very confidential. And when we had downed a third cup he was telling me things which I was certain he shouldn't.

"Such a to-do this morning," he confided, tapping the side of his nose with a delicate forefinger. "My lord—my lord of Gloucester, that is," he added, in case I was ignorant of the significance of the badge on his tunic, "arrives at his brother the Duke of Clarence's house with a demand to see Lady Anne. Lady Anne Neville, the late Earl of Warwick's daughter."

"I know," I said, unable to resist airing my knowledge. "I saw her last spring in Bristol, riding down Corn Street with Queen Margaret."

My acquaintance looked scandalized. "The Lady Margaret of Anjou," he corrected me in admonitory accents. "You must never refer to her nowadays as the

Queen." He put his head on one side, consideringly. "That must have been before the battle of Tewkesbury."

"A few days before," I agreed.

"Well," he continued, lowering his voice to an even more confidential whisper, "since then she's been staying with my lord of Clarence and his wife. The Duchess Isobel is her sister." Again I nodded, and again he appeared a little crestfallen by the extent of this country bumpkin's knowledge. "My lord of Gloucester wants to marry her. Naturally. They were childhood sweethearts years ago when my lord was an apprentice knight in Warwick's household at Middleham. But the Duke of Clarence, who's inherited all his late father-in-law's estates in right of his wife, can't bear the thought of parting with half of them."

"Understandably," I interrupted.

The little man snorted disparagingly. "He shouldn't have got anything at all, if you want my opinion, not after betraying his brothers like he did and supporting King Henry." I wondered idly why it was all right to refer to "King" Henry but not "Queen" Margaret, but I held my peace. The politics of those days were extremely complicated. My acquaintance continued: "Anyway, my lord appealed to the King, and the King told brother George that he was not to interfere with brother Richard's courtship, especially as Lady Anne herself seemed anxious for the marriage. So—" the little man leaned towards me across the table, his pale eyes gleaming with suppressed excitement, his breath, stinking with ale, fanning my cheek— "this morning as ever was, we ride out to call on Lady Anne. But when we get to my lord of Clarence's house, what do you think has happened?"

"I've no idea," I answered, shaking my head.

"She isn't there! And the Duke disclaims all knowledge of her whereabouts. He says she's simply disappeared!"

CHAPTER
15

Disappeared! That word seemed to have haunted me, both waking and sleeping, these past few months. First Clement Weaver, then Sir Richard Mallory and his servant, Jacob Pender. Now, here was a great lady of the realm gone missing. Not that there was anything I could do about that, but it was a strange coincidence, nevertheless. I drank some more ale and glanced sideways at the little man.

"What did my lord of Gloucester have to say about that?"

"He just answered quietly that he would find Lady Anne however long it took him to do so, and left. He's not one to rant and rave when crossed. His anger smoulders, never burns. He's not a true Plantagenet in that way." There was a tender note in my acquaintance's voice when he spoke of his master. It was obvious that he was devoted to the King's youngest brother, as, I suspected, were all the Duke's servants. I had noted the same look of loving respect in the eyes of his entourage who had protected him from the crowds yesterday morning. The people liked him, too.

"Do you think my lord of Clarence knows where Lady Anne is hidden?"

My question provoked a contemptuous glance. "Of course he knows! Don't imagine that she's disappeared of her own free will! She's being held somewhere on Clarence's orders. And somehow or other, he's persuaded Duchess Isobel that what he's doing is for her sister's good. George Plantagenet has always been a plausible rascal." The little man spat on the floor, making a wet patch in the sawdust. "But whatever he does, his brothers remain fond of him, particularly my own lord. Christ alone knows why! Clarence is a treacherous bastard."

I noted the swift progression from "plausible rascal" to "treacherous bastard" and connected it to an additional consumption of ale. My little man was getting too drunk for safety, both his and my own. There might be servants of Clarence in this alehouse—in this very room! I preferred not to be overheard criticizing the Duke, however indirectly.

"I must be going," I said, getting to my feet and hoisting up my pack. "Thank you for your hospitality."

"Thank you for saving me from that brute of a pieman." He, too, got up and bowed ceremoniously, but staggering slightly as he did so. His speech was clear and unslurred, but I felt, all the same, that it was time to go. I returned his bow and made my way out into East Cheap once more.

By mid-afternoon, I had sold all that was in my pack, and debated with myself whether to go straight to Galley Quay or wait until the next morning. There would be fresh ships in tomorrow, and in the meantime there might be shopkeepers willing to sell such items as needles and thread, ribbons and laces to me in quantity, reducing their prices accordingly. A third possibility was to declare the rest of the day a holiday. I had worked hard from early morning and had done well, earning more than enough to keep myself at the Baptist's Head for two or three days longer; sufficient, in fact, to insist on paying for my room and to stop imposing on Thomas Prynne's generosity.

It was, needless to say, the last choice which appealed to me most. I needed to clear my head and put the confused impressions of yesterday and today in some sort of order. And so that I could salve my slightly uneasy conscience, I decided to walk down by the river, along the wharfsides, heading in the general direction of Galley Quay. If, when I reached it, there was still merchandise to be bought of the kind that I needed, I could do so. Otherwise, I would return to The Street later in the day, just before the shops were stripped of their wares for the night, which would be stored under lock and key in the living quarters. It had been my experience that shopkeepers were more prone to strike a bargain when they were tired and looking forward to their suppers. I had grown craftier, I felt, now that I had passed the age of nineteen. (Four days before, while I was still on the road from Canterbury, it had been my Birth Day, although I had mentioned the fact to no one.) I realized that, in the past months, since leaving the Abbey and being on the road, I had truly become a man.

I made my way down to the river, where the gilded barges of the gentry sped along like great angry swans, imperiling lesser craft in their headlong flight. Watermen shouted abuse, crane operators paused in their work of unloading vessels moored at the wharves and people on the bank, including myself, stared somberly but without resentment at these symbols of a power we could not hope to attain. But then, I suppose we English have never really envied our nobles, because we have always believed in Justinian's maxim that what affects the people should be approved by the people, and throughout our history have taken steps, however slow and feeble, to ensure that this is so.

I emerged on to the quayside near London Bridge, close to a flight of water-steps, where a fleet of small boats, both uncovered (one penny) and covered (two pennies), were moored, waiting to ferry passengers up and down the river. A party of youths in satin and velvet tunics, with shoe-pikes so long that they had to be chained round their knees, were vying with a couple of more soberly dressed citizens for the attention of the boatmen.

"Wagge! Wagge! Go we hence!" the young men shouted, and the boatmen, rightly calculating that there was more money to be made in tips from them than the other two would-be customers, swarmed up the steps to offer their services.

I wandered on, threading my way in and out of the cranes and the workmen's huts on the wharfside, deliberately letting my mind empty of all thoughts of Clement Weaver and Sir Richard Mallory, and now, the missing Lady Anne Neville. For a while, at least, I would allow myself to think of nothing but the pleasant October afternoon and the delicious supper which Thomas Prynne was no doubt at that moment preparing.

A hand clutched my sleeve and a throaty voice said: "I thought it was you, Roger Chapman."

I was growing accustomed by now to hearing myself so addressed, although in my youth I had been known as Roger Carverson, or Carver for short, after my father's trade. I recognized the voice at once, without turning my head, as Philip Lamprey's.

"We meet again, then," I said, stating the obvious, and he agreed with a friendly grin.

"I told you, didn't I? London ain't that big."

I looked at him and noted that he was a little smarter than when I had seen him last, his patched and faded old woolen tunic having been replaced with one made of camlet. This was equally faded, and the grey squirrel fur which trimmed it had in places been rubbed right down to the skin. It also had a peculiar smell, as though at some time or another it had been next to a pile of rotting fish. In addition, it looked as though it had been immersed in water for a time and then roughly dried. All the same, the tunic was plainly of good quality, and the camlet—a mixture of wool and camel's hair, imported from the East— had survived the treatment meted out to it.

Philip saw me looking, and smiled. "Warmer than my old one," he said. "Niffs a bit, but then what d'you expect? Been in the Thames two or three weeks, old Bertha reckoned, when she fished it out along of its owner.

And it's been 'angin' up in 'er place, down by the river, over to Southwark, for nigh on a year. Askin' too much fer it, she was. 'Belonged to a gentleman,' she said. 'I ain't lettin' it go fer nothin'.' Though what she calls nothin' . . . But there, it's not an easy way to earn a livin', corpsing ain't. Pays better than beggin', but it wouldn't be my choice, even though I've seen enough dead bodies when I was a soldier."

I had never heard of "corpsing" then, but I could guess what it entailed. "You mean this woman, this Bertha, fishes dead bodies out of the Thames and sells their clothes?"

Philip Lamprey nodded. " 'S right. She don't do it single-'anded, o' course. 'Er 'usband and son do the fishin'. She jus' strips the corpses and dries the clothes before she sells 'em."

"And what happens to the poor unfortunates who owned the clothes? I don't imagine," I added drily, "that they're then given a decent Christian burial?"

My friend chuckled. "Lord bless you, no! They're just thrown back in the river, where they came from."

It was the answer I had foreseen. I suspected that the trade carried on by this Bertha and her family was unlawful, and she could hardly advertise it by seeking the assistance of a priest.

"And how were you able to afford this 'costly' garment?" I inquired ironically. "Have you suddenly become a rich man?"

My tone was lost on my companion. "I've 'ad my eye on it fer a while now," he confided. "And yesterday, I 'ad a good day. I got m'self a good position outside the Archbishop of York's 'ouse, near the Charing Cross,

'cause someone'd told me 'e was in London this week,
seein' the King. Meetin' of the Council, or whatever.
George Neville's quite a generous man, contrary to what
you might 'ave 'eard said of 'im.''

The name Neville made me wonder if the Archbishop was aware that his niece was missing, or even if he
was privy to her disappearance.

George Neville and George of Clarence had always
been as thick as thieves. Or, at least, so said the rumors
which had penetrated even our monastic walls.

I became aware that Philip Lamprey was still speaking. ". . . so I drove a 'ard bargain, and now it's mine.
Bertha was glad to get rid of it in the end, I think. It 'ad
been around too long. She usually shifts 'er stuff much
quicker. 'Ere,'' he added, nudging me in the ribs with
one of his sharp bony elbows, "there's initials embroidered in real gold thread up by the collar. See?'' He
tucked one hand inside the neckline of the tunic, making
a bulge in the material just below the grey fur border.

I peered closely and could just make out two letters,
or what was left of them, embroidered in tarnished gold
thread. C.W. My heart began thumping against my ribs.
C.W. Was it possible that this tunic had once belonged to
Clement Weaver?

I told myself not to be foolish. There were many names
which began with those letters. Nevertheless, I looked
carefully once again at the camlet tunic. The C and the W
had been intertwined, embellished with flourishes and
curlicues. Much of the thread was now missing, but I
could see by the needle-holes the original pattern. For

whoever embroidered it, it had been a labor of love; a mother? a sister? Alison Weaver?

"I think I may know the owner of this tunic," I said to Philip Lamprey. "Will you take me to see this Bertha?"

He looked dubious. "You ain't goin' to make a fuss about it, are you? You ain't thinkin' of callin' in the Law? Bertha's my friend. I don't want to get 'er into trouble."

"I just want to know exactly where she found the body."

Still he sucked his lower lip, unable to make up his mind regarding my intentions. "It's a long time ago. She may not be able to remember."

"Maybe not, but I'd like to ask her, all the same. If you won't take me, I'll find her myself. I'm sure she's quite well known on the Southwark side of the river."

With a sigh, Philip capitulated. "C'mon, then," he said. "But you'll 'ave to pay fer the ferry."

I was more than willing to do so, and we headed for the nearest water-stairs, where the inevitable fleet of boats was waiting. As it was a fine afternoon, we chose an uncovered one and were rowed across to the opposite shore with a gentle breeze blowing in our faces. The waters of the Thames were a little choppy, but the sun crested the waves with gold, and the glittering distances promised another good day tomorrow.

I had gained only the most fleeting impression of Southwark two evenings ago, when I had arrived there with my friends from Canterbury. And I had been up and gone very early the following morning, making my way across the Bridge to the city. But I had been warned of its reputation; of its bear-baiting pits, its cock-fighting rings, its stews and its brothels. It boasted, too, several churches, of which St. Mary Overy was the largest, and one or two fine mansions on its outskirts. I remembered one of the pilgrims pointing out a house to me which, he said, had once belonged to Sir John Fastolfe. He had also recommended to my notice the Tabard inn, made famous by Master Chaucer in his stories.

When we landed there were a number of whores in the striped hoods which were the badge of their profession waiting for a boat to take them across to the city.

"We 'ear the Archbishop of York's in town," one said to the boatman with a lecherous giggle.

Once again, I felt a stab of disapproval and shock that churchmen should consort with prostitutes, which made me realize, not for the first time, that I was neither so worldly-wise nor so world-weary as I liked to think myself.

I followed Philip Lamprey through a warren of narrow, filthy streets bordering the Thames, eventually emerging on to an abandoned wharf—Angel Wharf, so Philip informed me—a little way up river. Here, there was a settlement of near-derelict huts and hovels, occupied by what looked at first sight to be a tribe of beggars. A second, more searching look, however, told me that this was a permanent community, with its own boats moored alongside the wall, next to a shallow flight of well-worn steps leading up from the river. As Philip and I neared the entrance to the wharf an urchin seated on the ground and playing at five-stones gave us a piercing stare; then, apparently unconcerned, dropped his eyes again and continued with his game. But a few seconds later a shrill, ear-splitting whistle came from behind us, and I realized that he was warning of our approach. As we emerged from the dark, stinking alley into the afternoon sunshine, there was no one to be seen.

Had I gone alone to Angel Wharf, I should have accomplished nothing. Indeed, there is the possibility that I might never have been seen again. It was a sort of thieves' kitchen, where everyone made his or her living by working on the wrong side of the law; and where, as a consequence, strangers were viewed with the deepest suspicion. And people who had come to ask questions, like me, were the most mistrusted and unwelcome of all.

Philip Lamprey, however, seemed perfectly at ease and shouted: "Bertha! Bertha Mendip! It's me! Philip Lamprey!"

As though by magic, a number of the hovel doors opened and a few moments later the wharf was full of curious faces all staring in our direction. To begin with, no one came close, leaving us standing in the center of an empty circle, as if we were lepers. But finally, what looked like a bundle of evil-smelling rags detached itself from the ruck of onlookers, advanced a step or two and resolved itself into a tiny woman, thin almost to the point of emaciation, with shriveled features and a skin like leather. With a shock, I realized that the dirty, unkempt hair straggling about her shoulders was still a dark chestnut-brown and bore only a trace of grey. She had probably seen fewer than thirty-five summers, but appeared to be twice that age until I looked into her eyes. These were a brilliant blue, full of eagerness and life.

"Oo's this, then?" she demanded of Philip Lamprey.

"Friend o' mine." Philip plainly considered that sufficient introduction. " 'E wants to ask you about this 'ere tunic." And he indicated the garment he was wearing.

"Oh yes?" Bertha sounded unimpressed, and, just as plainly, my friendship with Philip did not inspire her with confidence. "Oo is 'e?"

"I've told you." Philip was impatient. "A friend. You can trust 'im."

There was an ugly murmur from the onlookers and I felt the hair rise on the nape of my neck. All I wanted to do was turn and run. Then I had a sudden inspiration. I remembered that Philip had called her Bertha Mendip.

"I'm a chapman," I said. "I was at Glastonbury Abbey as a novice until I decided that I didn't care for the monastic life. My home's in Wells. My father was a stone carver for the cathedral."

The tribal instinct is very strong in England, even today, in this enlightened new century. But fifty years or more ago, it was still stronger. The fact that I was a Somerset man born and bred in no way proved that I was trustworthy, yet Bertha Mendip accepted me immediately. She lost her aggressive attitude and jerked her head in the direction of one of the huts.

"You'd better come inside, then."

The interior of the hut stank with the smell of drying clothes which had been too long immersed in water and in contact with decaying flesh. They hung on poles at one end of the room, the smoke from a desultory fire curling through a hole in the ceiling. A young boy, presumably Bertha's son, as small and shriveled as she was, was throwing damp wood on to the blaze in an effort to keep it going. Of the husband mentioned by Philip there was no sign.

KATE SEDLEY · 196

"Well?" Bertha demanded truculently, as though angry with herself for accepting me so readily. "What is it you want to know?"

"Whereabouts in the Thames you found the body which wore that tunic," I answered, nodding towards Philip Lamprey.

She prevaricated. "It's a long time ago. More'n a year. For some reason, no one would buy it."

"You asked too much fer it, that's why," Philip interrupted. "It's all right. You can trust 'im. 'E's jus' tryin' to find a friend oo disappeared last winter from outside the Crossed 'Ands inn. No one knows if this young man is alive or dead, an' it's 'ard on 'is family."

I had, inevitably, been forced, on our way here to satisfy Philip's rampant curiosity regarding my interest in the camlet tunic, and so had told him my story, or such parts of it as were relevant to our mission. I prayed devoutly that I should not now have to repeat it yet again for Bertha Mendip, but fortunately, Philip's explanation seemed to satisfy her. She thought deeply for a moment or two, then nodded.

"In that case," she said at last, "per'aps I do remember. Come outside with me, both of you, an' I'll point out the spot to you. And Matt! You keep that fire going!" she admonished her son. "D'you 'ear me?"

The boy nodded sullenly, and I noted that, for all his thinness, he had a strong, wiry frame, and that what I had assumed to be twigs, because he snapped them so easily, were really quite substantial branches. I smiled at him, but elicited no response other than a scowl. He was obviously deeply suspicious of strangers, even of those approved of by his mother. Abandoning my attempt at friendliness, I followed Bertha and Philip out of the hut and joined them where they were standing at the wharf-side.

CHAPTER

16

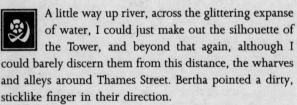 A little way up river, across the glittering expanse of water, I could just make out the silhouette of the Tower, and beyond that again, although I could barely discern them from this distance, the wharves and alleys around Thames Street. Bertha pointed a dirty, sticklike finger in their direction.

"Up there, it were. Close to the shore. Body of a young man which 'ad got trapped in a fisherman's net. It 'appens sometimes. In fact, 'e were the third what I'd caught near there."

I digested this piece of information. "Were all the bodies fully clothed?"

Bertha nodded. "No ornaments of any kind on 'em mind you, but you wouldn't expect that, not if they'd been robbed, which most of 'em 'ad been. Sometimes, o' course, you find corpses what've still got their rings on and their gold chains round their necks, and you thanks God for 'em. Drunks oo've fallen in the river at night, or people oo've fallen overboard from boats, 'specially after some fool's tried 'is 'and at shootin' the arches.'' These, I guessed to be the arches of London Bridge, through which the current swirled so dangerously at ebb tide. Bertha continued: ''But most of 'em, as I say, are poor bastards what've been set on and killed for the few paltry coins in their purses.''

I found Bertha's sympathy for the victims she then stripped and threw back in the river macabre, but was careful not to show my revulsion. ''This young man,'' I asked, ''who was wearing the camlet tunic, how old would you say he was?''

''I told you,'' she answered impatiently, '' 'e were a young man.'' She eyed me up and down. ''Your age maybe. An' 'e 'adn't been in the water long when I found 'im. Fishes 'adn't started nibblin' at 'im.''

I felt my stomach heave and was afraid that I was going to be sick. But I managed to swallow my nausea and, after a moment or two, was able to ask in a steady voice: ''Would this have been around All Hallows'-tide?''

Bertha considered, chewing a black fingernail between broken teeth. ''Could've been,'' she admitted slowly. ''Ye-es. It could've been. The nights were drawin' in, as I remember. It was gettin' dark early.'' She thought for a little longer. ''It 'ad been bad weather. Rainin' for several days before'and. It was a nasty black night and still rainin' when I found 'im.''

"Was that anywhere near the entrance to Crooked Lane?" I prompted, after she had fallen silent.

"Little way down river from there, but not far. The current 'adn't 'ad a chance carry 'im any distance because of the fishing net, like I told you."

"These other two bodies you found near there, was that before or after the one we're talking about?"

Bertha stopped biting her nail and sucked her teeth.

"The first was a long time ago," she replied eventually. "As for the other, I can't rightly remember. One body looks much like another after it's been in the river a while. They all get muddled up in my mind."

I thanked her courteously for her help and indicated to Philip Lamprey that it was time to go. I should be thankful to quit Angel Wharf. It made the flesh crawl along my bones.

"Do you think it's the young man you're lookin' for?" Bertha asked me.

"Yes, almost certainly. When I see his family again, I shall tell them to give up hope." I was about to move away when a thought struck me. "You know London well," I said. "Why is that alley called Crooked Lane? There's no bend in it."

Bertha once more sucked her teeth, which seemed to be her habit when she was thinking. "Wasn't always called that," she answered after a while. "When I was a child it 'ad a different name, as I recall . . . Doll!" she shrieked, and another woman, older than herself, appeared in the door of a nearby hovel. "Didn't Crooked Lane, in Thames Street, used to be called somethin' else?"

"Conduit Lane," the other woman answered shortly, and went inside again.

"Tha's it." Bertha nodded sagely. "Don't ask me 'ow it came to change its name, 'cos I don't know, and that's a fact."

I could see that mispronunciation over a number of years could have wrought the transformation, until common usage had turned "Conduit" into "Crooked," but there was no conduit in the street, either. I said as much, and once again Doll was summoned.

"Why was it called Conduit Lane?" Bertha demanded.

At first, it seemed that Doll was unable to remember, or perhaps had never known the reason. But eventually, after much questioning, not only by Bertha, Philip Lamprey and myself, but also by other occupants of Angel Wharf who had started to take an interest in the proceedings, she said she thought there was an underground drain which ran from the cellars of one of the inns and emptied into the river. It had been used, although exactly how Doll was unsure, to smuggle untaxed casks of wine on to the premises.

And that, I could see, was as much as Doll could tell us, but even so, my heart was thumping with excitement. If that underground drain still existed, as it probably did, between the river and the Crossed Hands inn, and even if it was no longer used for its original purpose, it still offered a simple way of disposing of dead bodies.

But why were there dead bodies in the first place? Why had Clement Weaver been murdered, as I was now sure he had been? And had the same fate overtaken Sir Richard Mallory and Jacob Pender? And what, if anything, did it all have to do with the mysterious young woman who seemed to be a virtual prisoner of Martin Trollope?

To none of these questions did I as yet have a satisfactory answer.

I thanked Bertha again and followed Philip Lamprey back to the water-stairs near London Bridge, where we crossed once more by boat to the city. It was now late in the afternoon, getting near supper-time, and I was hungry. I needed sustenance and time to put my thoughts in order. So much had happened during the past two days that I was in danger of becoming confused enough to do nothing. I was as sure now as I would ever be that Clement Weaver was dead, so why pursue the matter? As I walked from the Bridge along Thames Street, having said my farewells to Philip Lamprey, who was anxious by this time to go about his own business, I asked myself that question. But I already knew the answer. God had given me yet more proof that it was His will that I should unravel this mystery. Try as I might, I was unable to convince myself that Philip Lamprey's purchase of the camlet tunic after all these months, and our subsequent meeting, was simply coincidence. God's Hand was here, and I could not ignore it. Moreover, some sixth sense told me that all the necessary pieces to solve the puzzle were in front of me, if only I had eyes to see them. I recalled the nagging sensation I had experienced, on more than one occasion, that I had missed something vital; something someone had either said or done, but which I had found it impossible to recapture.

So what choice did I have, but to continue with my quest? Perhaps inspiration would come to me when I had food inside me.

* * *

As I rounded the corner of Crooked Lane, by the Crossed Hands inn, I could see a great deal of bustle in the courtyard. A lady wrapped in a fur-trimmed cloak was being helped to alight from a traveling wagon, while a gentleman, equally richly dressed and presumably her husband, was giving the ostlers precise instructions as to the stabling of his horses. Martin Trollope himself was much in evidence to welcome his obviously distinguished guests, and quite a few of the inn's servants were on display to create the right impression. In fact, so much attention was being concentrated on the new arrivals that it occurred to me I might enter the inn and no one would even notice me. Putting my theory to the test, I slipped my empty pack from my back just inside the archway, walked quietly past Martin Trollope, so close that I almost touched him, mounted the stairs to the balcony and let myself in through the door at the far end.

All was as quiet here as it had been on my previous visit; no sign of any servants going about their duties, only a silence which, to my over-stretched imagination, seemed deeply menacing. Stealthily I tried the latch of the door on my left, but this time it did not open. I pushed again, gently, but it was bolted from inside.

I crossed to the window opposite, set it wide and leaned out, twisting my neck until I could see down into the courtyard. There, all was as before, with Martin Trollope still attending to the orders and wishes of the new arrivals and two of the servants now unloading a large traveling chest from the back of the wagon. I withdrew my head and quietly closed the casement. If the gentleman's loud, blustering tones, and his lady's softer, but equally penetrating whine were anything to judge by, they would be the focus of attention for some time to come. I crossed back to the door and once more tried the latch, but it remained unyielding.

I put my lips to the crack between the door and its jamb and whispered as loudly as I dared: "Is anyone in there?"

There was a long silence before I heard the faintest of movements, like the rustle of a woman's gown as it brushed against the rushes on the floor. I whispered again, only this time a little louder: "Is anyone in there?"

I was rewarded by a slight cough, but once more, this sign of life was succeeded by silence. I rattled the latch carefully, then decided on a change of tactics. "Don't be afraid," I said. "I'm not one of the inn servants. I'm a friend. I want to help you."

Again I heard the rustle of skirts, then a faint breathing on the other side of the door. "Who are you?" asked a woman's voice, rapid and low, as though afraid that we might be discovered at any moment. "What's your name?"

"My name's Roger. I'm a chapman. I think I saw you at the window yesterday morning. I thought . . . I don't know why, but I thought you might be in trouble. Held against your will . . . If I'm being foolish, say so."

Another long pause followed my words, before the same voice whispered: "Can I really trust you?"

But I had only just time enough to whisper back: "Absolutely!" before there was a footfall on the little, twisting stair at the end of the corridor and one of the inn's chambermaids appeared, carrying a pile of clean linen, evidently destined for the room where my prisoner was held.

"What do you want?" she demanded. "Does the master know that you're here?"

I thought quickly. "I'm looking for one of the guests," I said. "A Master Gilbert Parsons. This is the Baptist's Head hostelry, isn't it?"

"No, it's down the street a pace. This is the Crossed Hands inn." The girl snorted derisively. "Master Trollope wouldn't thank you for mistaking that poky place for this. Now, be off with you! Before," she added shrewdly, "I bother to find out if you're lying or not."

I had no choice but to leave, cursing my bad luck. I sensed that even if I hung around the inn and waited until the coast was clear again, I should get nothing more from my captive. She had been nervous enough before the interruption: she would be doubly so now. So I thanked the chambermaid with a winning smile, and let myself out through the balcony door. Down in the courtyard nothing much had changed. The loud-voiced gentleman and his insistently complaining wife were still claiming all Martin Trollope's attention, and as I paused to catch my breath before making my escape, I heard the woman say: "My lord of Clarence himself recommended this inn to us on the last occasion he was our guest in Devonshire. He would be displeased to know that we are being offered an inferior bedchamber at the back of the house."

"Quite right! Quite right, my dear!" Her husband endorsed these sentiments with a beefy slap on Master Trollope's shoulder. "Turn someone else out, if necessary, landlord! We shouldn't like to have to complain to His Grace, but if needs must . . ."

The rest of his words were lost to me as I was struck by a blinding light. St. Paul on the road to Damascus did not receive so great a revelation as came to me then, standing on the balcony of the Crossed Hands inn. I knew who was hidden in that room, even without seeing her face. But I had seen it, of that I was certain; in Corn Street, in Bristol, five months ago. I recalled what Bess Woodward had said to me; that Martin Trollope was the cousin of a dependant of the Duke of Clarence. And with that recollection came the memory of Philip Lamprey's words: "I did over'ear someone say as 'ow 'e was a greedy bastard. Willin' to do anythink fer money." Thomas Prynne had told me: "A great deal of trade at the Crossed Hands is by recommendation of the Duke himself. I wish I could boast as much in the way of royal support."

So Martin Trollope owed my lord of Clarence many favors. The Crossed Hands inn would therefore be the natural place for the latter to choose if he wanted to hide his sister-in-law from his brother. Who would think of looking for one of the highest born ladies of the realm in a common inn, disguised as a cookmaid? Not that I imagined Lady Anne had been allowed anywhere near the kitchens, but it would have been impossible to keep her presence a complete secret from the other servants. Hence the story that the new girl was ill and had to stay in her room. How long this falsehood could be perpetuated it was difficult to guess, but no doubt the Duke of Clarence had made further arrangements for Lady Anne's concealment if anyone at the Crossed Hands became suspicious. But he had reckoned without me, the outsider.

I slipped quietly down the stairs, passed once again within an inch of Martin Trollope's back, grabbed my pack and stick and was out into Crooked Lane without giving myself time to think of the danger. Then, my heart thudding against my ribs, I made my way thankfully to the safety of the Baptist's Head to consult Thomas Prynne.

"You're sure of your facts, lad? Absolutely certain?"

I didn't blame Thomas Prynne or Abel Sampson for not entirely believing me. I found the situation difficult to believe myself, so I had not overstretched their credulity by repeating my other suspicions regarding Martin Trollope and the Crossed Hands inn. I knew now what I was going to do about that, but there was the rescue of Lady Anne to be accomplished first.

There were still a few hours left before curfew. The early October day had latterly been a fine one and no obscuring clouds added to the encroaching darkness. I had eaten hurriedly at the kitchen table while telling my story to my two hosts, and regretting, busy as my mind was with other things, that I could not do more justice to Thomas's cooking. Beneath their initial reluctance to accept my story, I could sense interest and excitement at such events happening in their neighborhood. There was an air of tension in the kitchen.

"Where will I find the Duke of Gloucester?" I asked them.

Abel glanced at Thomas and raised his eyebrows. "I believe that when in London he lodges with his mother, the Dutchess of York, at Baynard's Castle."

Thomas nodded in agreement.

"Where's that?" I asked him.

"Not far from the Steelyard, fronting on to the river.

It belonged once to the Black Friars and that part of the city still bears their name."

"I think I've seen it," I said. "A great house with battlements and towers."

Once again Thomas nodded, but he was beginning to look apprehensive. "You're sure you know what you're doing, lad? The Duke won't thank you if you lead him on a wild goose chase. You're positive that the Lady Anne Neville is missing?"

"I had the story from one of the Duke's own servants. I explained that to you just now."

I must have sounded as impatient as I felt, because Abel said sharply: "There's no need to lose your temper. Thomas is only trying to stop you making a fool of yourself. According to your story, you haven't actually seen this woman who's supposed to be hidden at the Crossed Hands inn."

I swallowed my irritation, realizing that both he and his partner were only preaching caution for my own good. "I'm sorry," I said contritely, "but I'm as certain as I can be that she's the Lady Anne, and if I don't go to my lord of Gloucester with my information, such as it is, I feel I should be failing in my duty." Although why I should feel a greater sense of duty towards one royal brother than the other was something I could not explain, even to myself. Perhaps it was to do with being born on the same day; or with the immediate sense of affection which the young Duke had inspired in me the previous morning, when I had watched him ride past St. Paul's. And then, everyone spoke well of the King's youngest brother, while few had a good word to say for my lord of Clarence. But whatever the reason, my loyalty to, and my

CHAPTER
17

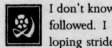I don't know exactly when I realized I was being followed. I had not hurried, going at an easy loping stride, because I had no wish to arrive at Baynard's Castle flustered and out of breath. I should need to keep my wits about me, be calm and authoritative, if I was to stand any chance of seeing the Duke. As I made my way along Thames Street, still crowded at this time of the afternoon, I prayed that he would not be from home.

It was in the vicinity of the Bridge, where Fish Street runs northward towards East Cheap and the Bishop's Gate, that I happened to glance behind me. It was chance that I did so: a shout or a noise of some kind had attracted my attention, but before I could locate its source or satisfy my curiosity, I was aware of a slight, hooded figure moving swiftly through the crowds in my wake. Even then, I should have taken no notice of it but for the fact that, as soon as I turned my head, the cloaked figure dodged hurriedly between two stalls and disappeared from view.

The person had been half-walking, half-running at such a rate and with such purpose that this sudden vanishing act intrigued me. Moreover, there was something familiar about the figure; the movement, the flow of the long cloak, the hood pulled well forward, concealing the face. Then it came to me. It was the man, or woman, I had seen in the early hours of this morning, hurrying up Crooked Lane and entering the Crossed Hands inn.

I continued on my way in the same steady fashion for several minutes, before turning my head for the second time. The cloaked figure was still there and had gained on me, so that I could now see skirts beneath the hem of the cloak. A woman, then! But who? The answer sprang to mind almost at once. Matilda Ford, Marjorie Dyer's cousin. My presence at the Crossed Hands inn must, after all, have been noticed. Either that, or the chambermaid had mentioned our meeting to Martin Trollope. He, suspicious, had set Matilda to watch the Baptist's Head, and when informed that I had set out again, had instructed her to follow. I was some way ahead by that time, and she had been forced to hurry in order to catch me up.

When I glanced back at her again, she immediately slowed her pace, pausing to inspect the remaining wares displayed on a butcher's slab. I saw the man speak to her, but she shook her head and moved on slowly. I resumed my walking, but a few seconds later looked over my shoulder a third time, to find that she had nearly caught

up with me. We had passed the entrance to London
Bridge, and the crowds here were thinning as people finished their day's marketing and began making their way
home for the night. One or two shopkeepers were start-
ing to carry their goods inside, although most continued
to shout their wares, still hoping to attract last-minute
custom.

I continued on my way, debating with myself how
best to deal with the situation. Should I simply carry on as
though unaware of her presence? Or should I turn and
confront her? But how would she respond to my challenge? And what did Martin Trollope hope to gain by
having a woman follow me? She could do me no harm
. . . I cursed myself for a slow-witted fool. Matilda Ford
did not need to harm me. As soon as she saw where I was
going, she would return hot-foot to the Crossed Hands
inn and Lady Anne would at once be spirited away. The
only thing I could do was to give her the slip.

But how? The towers of Baynard's Castle were already looming ahead of me. If I didn't act quickly, Matilda would guess my destination and return at once to
inform Martin Trollope . . . A woman in a striped hood
loomed out of the shadows, and a hand caressed my
shoulder.

"Looking for someone, my pretty ducks?"

I have been called many names in my time, some apt
and well-deserved, others less so. But "pretty ducks" is,
perhaps, the least fitting of them all to describe my bulk
and height. Nevertheless, the woman was a godsend.
(And after all, if God used the Magdalene for his purposes, why not other whores? I asked myself.) I slipped

one arm around her waist and was pleasantly surprised to find that she smelled quite clean.

"Where . . . Where do you—er—work?"

She laughed at that and jerked her head in the direction of a narrow alley. "Old Mother Bindloss's, in Pudding Street. Come on. It's just along 'ere."

Resisting the temptation to see if Matilda Ford was watching, I allowed myself to be led into the alley. The stench of putrefaction met my nostrils, and I noticed that the drain running down the middle of the street was full to overflowing, a dead cat and several dead rats among the rotting food and human excrement. London streets in general are not very clean, but this was particularly noisome. My companion stopped half way along at one of the houses and rapped on the door.

A grid in the top of the door was opened and a voice inquired: "Who is it?"

"Susan," the girl answered in a sibilant whisper. "I've got a customer."

I could no longer resist looking back along the street, and was just in time to note Matilda Ford disappearing quickly round the corner. She had evidently been watching to see where I went. I trusted that she was now satisfied and had not divined my real intentions.

The door was opened and I stepped inside, prompted by a push from Susan. A guttering candle illuminated a narrow passageway and a flight of stairs, on which were seated a number of girls in various states of undress.

"Hell's teeth!" one of them exclaimed, craning her neck eagerly over the heads of the others. "Where did you find him? Hey, sweetheart! When you've finished with Susan, I'm willin'! I'm sure a big boy like you has more than one fuck in 'im.''

There was a ragged cheer from the other women and, to my horror, I found myself blushing. Fortunately, it was too dark for them to see. I turned to my companion.

"I'm sorry," I said, fumbling in the purse at my belt and producing a silver penny, "but I don't want your . . . your services." Susan stared at me, uncomprehending. "Look," I went on quickly, pressing the coin into her hand, "I'm willing to pay for your time and trouble. But the truth is, I only came in here to shake off the woman who was following me.". I added lamely: "I'm afraid I can't explain more than that."

"Your wife, is it?" asked the girl who had spoken first. "And you're sloping off to meet another woman?"

There was a sympathetic murmur from the others. Even Susan, who had been looking deeply affronted, smiled and patted my shoulder.

" 'Ere you are, sweet'eart, you keep your money. And if your ladylove don't want you after all, come back 'ere and we'll entertain you."

There were cries of agreement all round as I opened the door and slipped once more into the street. Thanking my unwitting savior with a blushing kiss on the cheek, I made my way back again towards the river. I did not hear her close the door behind me and suspected that she was watching my progress, regretting having let me go so easily. I glanced over my shoulder and saw that I was right. Susan was still standing in the open doorway . . .

It was at that moment, while my attention was distracted, that I felt, rather than saw, the sudden flurry of

movement ahead of me. I jerked my head round only just
in time to ward off the blow. Matilda Ford, arm raised,
had emerged from one of the doorways, where she had
been hiding, and was coming at me with a knife.

Instinctively, I grasped my stick in both hands and managed, but only just, to parry the blow. She was momentarily thrown off balance, but recovered quickly and came
at me again, as agile as a cat. The upraised blade of the
long, sharp knife, which I had seen her using to skin
rabbits in the Crossed Hands kitchen, glittered evilly in
the darkness of the alley. Again, I parried its downward
thrust, but in trying to side-step and avoid her next on-
slaught, I slipped on a piece of offal and went sprawling
to the ground. Frantically, I struggled to regain my feet,
but she was too swift for me, and out of the corner of my
eye I saw her moving in for the kill. The hood had fallen
back from her face and I could see it plainly, the lips
drawn back from the broken teeth, the eyes glittering
balefully, the nostrils flared, as though scenting blood. I
had never before come across so evil a woman. And it
looked as though it would be my first and last encounter.
With a grunt of desperation, I rolled to one side, trying to
avoid the knife.

I had no real hope of doing so. Almost in a dream, I
watched the flash of its downward arc . . . Nothing
happened. After what seemed an eternity, but was in fact
only a few brief seconds, I opened my eyes; eyes which,
like most people, I had shut in the face of certain death. I
was suddenly conscious of a babel of female voices;
shouts and imprecations, oaths and swear words which I

had never heard before in my life. As I scrambled to my feet, I saw Matilda Ford struggling in the clutches of a group of whores, led by Susan, who, by dint of biting her wrist, had forced Matilda to drop the knife. As I stooped to retrieve it, there was the sound of rending cloth, and, a moment later the noise of running feet told me that my would-be murderess had escaped, leaving only her torn cloak behind.

"Let her go!" I said quickly. "And thank you all for saving my life."

"Cor!" one of the girls exclaimed, her naked breasts heaving with exertion. "What a virago! Whatever made you marry her?"

I had temporarily forgotten my claim that I was being followed by my wife, but seized thankfully on the explanation. I must get to Baynard's Castle as swiftly now as possible. I had no wish to institute a hue and cry.

"Oh, you know how it is," I shrugged. "People change. And I dare say I've given her cause to be bitter. I must be on my way now. My—er—my mistress will be wondering what's become of me. Thank you all again."

I was sped on my way amid a chorus of ribald comments, the most innocuous of which was: "Give 'er one for me!" At the entrance to the alley, I paused to look carefully left and right, making sure that there was no sign of Matilda Ford, before turning to give my rescuers a farewell wave. Then, somewhat shaken, but still purposeful, I began walking rapidly in the direction of Baynard's Castle.

* * *

The sentries on the gate refused to let me pass. They were agreed that both my lord of Gloucester and Duchess Cicely were within, but it was more than their jobs were worth to admit a stranger so near to curfew. This was the time of day the Duke relaxed and entertained his guests. It was also the hour, when staying with his mother, which he devoted to his children, Lady Katherine and the little Lord John.

"If you've got a request," one sentry told me roughly, "come back tomorrow. My lord's holding a Court of Petition in the morning."

"It's not a request," I answered impatiently. "At least, tell the Duke I'm here! The matter is urgent."

Both men burst out laughing. "And who do you think you are, my jumped-up cocky?" the taller one asked, while the shorter said menacingly: "We don't let any poor bastard in off the street who's deluded enough to think he has something of importance to say to His Grace. Besides, for all we know, you might have a knife hidden under that cloak."

I held my cloak open so that they could see I was innocent of weapons—only to remember too late that when I had picked up Matilda Ford's knife, I had stuck it in my belt for safe-keeping. At the sight of it, unsheathed, both sentries seized me and dragged me inside.

Well, at least I was in, but not quite in the manner I had foreseen. Vociferously, I protested my good intentions, trying to drown my captors' shouts for assistance. I wondered how on earth I was going to convince them that I was not a would-be assassin. I sent up a desperate prayer for help. Surely God could not desert me now.

He didn't. The first man to arrive on the scene in

answer to the sentries' summons was the man I had rescued from the over-zealous pieman.

"What's going on?" he asked indignantly. "This noise can be heard in His Grace's private apartments. I hope there's a good explanation . . ." His voice tailed off as he recognized me. "What are you doing here?" he demanded.

The shorter sentry, who had just been about to brand me as a suspected criminal, hesitated. "Do you know him?" he asked my little man.

"We have a brief acquaintance," my friend was beginning, but I interrupted him urgently.

"I have to see the Duke. At once! I think I've found Lady Anne Neville."

To say his mouth fell open would not be too much of an exaggeration. His lower jaw almost touched his collar. "You're sure of this?" he demanded sharply.

It was my turn to hesitate. If I told the truth and admitted that I had not seen the lady face to face, I might again be suspected of bad intentions. Besides, in my own mind, I was completely certain. So I took a deep breath and said: "Yes. I know where the Lady Anne is hidden."

The little man turned to the sentries. "Let him go," he ordered. "I'll vouch for him." And to me, he added: "Come this way!"

The sentries reluctantly stood aside, having relieved me of both my stick and the knife. They were still unconvinced and deeply suspicious. I gave them what I hoped was a reassuring smile, and followed my guide across the outer courtyard and through a door to the inner, which housed the bakehouse, laundry and kitchens. The wall torches, high up in their iron sconces, had already been lit, flaring against the old stones with a noise like torn parchment. In this courtyard there was far more hustle and bustle; a constant whirl of activity and chatter, without which the great and the mighty seem unable to live. Men and boys in the livery of the Duke of Gloucester scurried self-importantly about, without ever, or so it appeared to my jaundiced eyes, actually achieving anything.

I was led up a narrow stone staircase, along an equally narrow passage, up another twisting stair, all the time having to flatten myself against the wall as people forced their way past me. My little friend was growing impatient at the delay, and finally cried out: "Holla! Holla! Make room! Make room! We are about the Lord Richard's business!" I can't say it had an instantaneous effect, but our progress did speed up a little. Finally we reached an archway shrouded by a leather curtain, which when pulled back, revealed an ante-chamber. Into this, I was ceremoniously ushered. I had a feeling that the little man was enjoying his moment of glory.

A young man, seated behind a table and busy with important-looking documents, raised his head inquiringly as we entered. My friend hissed in my ear: "John Kendal, His Grace's secretary."

"What can I do for you, Timothy Plummer?" John Kendal asked. "And who's this you have with you?"

"His name's Roger Chapman and he has very important news for the Duke."

The secretary's eyebrows rose in patent disbelief and he looked me up and down. I returned his gaze as steadily as I could in the face of such unnerving scrutiny. But he evidently liked what he saw, because he smiled suddenly and nodded.

"What might this news be, Roger Chapman? And I warn you, it will have to be very important indeed for His Grace to see you at this hour. It is the time of day he spends with his mother and children."

"He'll see me all right," I answered boldly. "I think I know the whereabouts of Lady Anne Neville."

The room into which I was shown was not a large one, but it was luxurious. A fire of scented pine logs burned on the hearth, and the rushes on the floor were mixed with an abundance of dried flowers. There were at least three armchairs, their backs delicately carved with patterns of birds and intertwined leaves, and four or five joint stools. A low table against one wall supported a silver ewer and goblets of fine Venetian glass, which winked and glowed in the firelight. The walls were hung with tapestries depicting the fight of Hercules with Nereus, first as a stag, then as bird, dog, snake and, finally, as a man. A myriad wax candles—or so it seemed to my dazzled eyes—hung in a copper chandelier from the ceiling.

Two children, a girl and a slightly younger boy, were playing on a rug—something I had never seen before—in front of the fire, and I knew they must be the Duke's two bastards. Seated in one of the armchairs, also close to the hearth, was a formidable-looking woman with strongly marked features. This, without doubt, was the Duchess of York, mother of the King and the Dukes of Gloucester and Clarence, sister of the late Earl of Warwick, and mother-in-law of the Duke of Burgundy. And, if all stories were true, an extremely redoubtable lady.

Duke Richard himself was on his feet as I entered. He was wearing a long, loose robe of dark red, sable-trimmed velvet, with black satin slippers heavily embroidered in gold thread. He was obviously resting after the cares of the day, and had it been for any other reason, I should have felt guilty at disturbing him. His thin face was sallow in the flickering candlelight, and there were dark shadows beneath his eyes, as though he had been sleeping badly. I learned later that the Countess of Desmond had once described him as the handsomest man in London, after his brother Edward. He certainly did not look it that night, but he was a man whose physical appearance was very much dependent on his state of health and the peace, or otherwise, of his state of mind.

He had been informed by John Kendal of the reason for my visit, and I could sense the tension in that slender body as I approached and made my obeisance. He held out a hand, prismatic with rings, for me to kiss.

"I understand," he said in a voice which was slightly breathless, "that you have some idea where my cousin, the Lady Anne Neville, might be. If that is so, tell me at once. If you should prove to be wrong, no harm will befall you. But first, tell me how you knew that she was missing."

I stood upright, dwarfing his slight, dark figure, but he was used to that. Both his remaining brothers were big, golden-haired men.

"Your Grace," I said, "that is part of a story which, with your permission, I will tell you as briefly as possible, because I need your help for my own purposes, once you have rescued the Lady Anne. If you will be gracious enough to hear me out."

He hesitated, clearly anxious to know only one thing, but his natural courtesy overcame his impatience. He sat down in one of the other two armchairs and indicated that I should begin.

CHAPTER

18

 "Sit down, lad, and have some wine. You look exhausted." Thomas Prynne urged me to a seat in the ale-room, where Master Parsons, his legal worries temporarily forgotten, was regarding me goggle-eyed. "I presume this hullabaloo at the Crossed Hands inn has something to do with you? His Grace of Gloucester seemed very friendly before you parted company."

Master Parson's look was now a blend of curiosity and awe. I had suddenly ceased to be a common chapman and become instead a person on friendly terms with a royal duke. Abel Sampson, who had followed us into the ale-room, also accorded me a new respect, while Thomas was as good as his word, and brought me a cup of his finest Bordeaux wine, drawn from a barrel in the cellar.

"Tell us the whole story," Abel commanded, putting another log on the fire, then drawing up a stool to join us at the table.

Thomas nodded. "You seem to have been right about that place."

I sipped my wine a little disconsolately. "Partly," I agreed, "but not wholly. There seems nothing to connect Martin Trollope or the inn with Clement Weaver's disappearance. Nor, indeed, with Sir Richard Mallory's, except for the fact that he and his man, Jacob Pender, stayed there. The Duke's men searched the house from top to bottom, but found nothing."

Abel Sampson shrugged. "You wouldn't expect to find anything, surely? All evidence would have been destroyed."

He was right, of course; but there had been something about Martin Trollope's protestations of innocence on that score which, despite my disinclination to believe him, had nevertheless convinced me. And there had been no sign of any conduit leading from the cellars down to the river. The Duke's men had searched long and hard, even calling for picks to be brought and hacking at the walls, but all to no avail. Why this seemed of such importance to me, I had no idea: there were other ways of disposing of dead bodies, after all. It was just an instinct; an intuition which had possessed me ever since I had heard the conduit mentioned by Bertha's friend, Doll.

Thomas Prynne replenished my glass, which by now was half-empty, and once again urged that I tell my story. Suppressing my disappointment, and the feeling that I had but half a tale to tell, I complied, adding to what the two partners already knew and ending with the discovery of Lady Anne Neville at the Crossed Hands inn.

"She was being held there against her will?" Abel Sampson asked incredulously.

I sipped my wine carefully, determined not to drink too much, but unwilling to give my hosts offence by appearing to drink too little. I nodded.

"Although," I added fair-mindedly, after giving the subject some thought, "perhaps that might be overstating the matter. She was not locked in, nor bound. The Duke of Clarence had placed her there, under the pretence of being a new cookmaid, to hide her from Duke Richard, who wants to marry her. Had she been made of sterner stuff, she could probably have walked free at any moment. I doubt very much if Martin Trollope would have dared use force to detain her."

"Then why in God's Name didn't she leave?" asked Master Parsons.

I shrugged. "A number of reasons, I should imagine. She is young and the Duke of Clarence is her guardian. It would be natural in her to obey him, even if she doesn't agree with his orders. Then the Duchess of Clarence is her older sister, and the two have always, or so I understand from those who know, been very close. And the Duchess would naturally uphold her husband. Whatever her natural inclinations or desires, Lady Anne would be afraid, possibly, to flout the wishes of two so close to her, particularly as her father was an attainted rebel."

Master Parsons, anxious to air his knowledge, agreed with me sagely. "And she has been through much this past year, poor child. The Earl's sudden defection to Queen Margaret and her cause, after a lifetime's loyalty to

King Edward; her enforced marriage to that young bully and braggart, Edward of Lancaster; his death on the field at Tewkesbury; being put, maybe against her will, into the custody of her sister and brother-in-law; all these things would have served to intimidate her."

Abel Sampson peered into my cup and saw that the level of my wine was still very near the top. He smote me on the shoulder. "Drink up, lad! Drink up! You deserve the pleasure of getting drunk, tonight of all nights!"

His partner frowned reprovingly at him. "Let the lad be, Abel! So what has my lord of Gloucester done with the lady, now that he's found her?"

"Escorted her to the sanctuary of St. Martin-le-Grand, where, so he told me, she will remain in safety until such time as he can win both his brothers' consent to their marriage."

Abel grimaced at Thomas, and a little of the mocking tone he had used towards me earlier crept back into his voice. " 'So he told me!' " he mimicked, and sighed gustily. "What it is to be the confidant of royalty!"

I felt the color stain my cheeks. Thomas saw it, too, and squeezed my arm. "Take no notice of him, lad! Envy has always been Abel's besetting sin. You've done well and deserve Duke Richard's thanks. Did he offer to reward you?"

I shook my head. "I did no more than my duty." But although I said nothing, I would never forget the warmth with which the Duke had pressed my hand on parting, as he prepared to leave the Crossed Hands inn to escort his cousin to sanctuary, nor the words which had accompanied the gesture.

"I shall remember the service you have rendered

me, Roger Chapman. If there is anything I can do for you, any assistance I can offer you at any time, you have only to send me word.''

Lady Anne, mounted in front of him on the big white horse and wrapped in his fur-lined cloak, had also shyly murmured her gratitude and given me her hand to kiss.

I had bowed as gallantly as I knew how. ''Your Grace has already repaid your debt by ordering your men to search the house.''

The Duke had pulled down the corners of his wide, thin mouth. ''To little purpose, I'm afraid. But I shall be keeping watch on Master Trollope in the future, and if I find evidence of any murderous activities, I shall instigate all necessary action, you have my word. I shall take a personal interest in the case. That rogue is capable of anything.''

Thomas Prynne's voice cut across these thoughts. ''You haven't told us what became of Matilda Ford. After her attack on you, didn't she return to Martin Trollope and warn him that she had been unsuccessful?''

I took another sip of wine and felt the warmth course along my veins; liquid fire relaxing the body.

''It would seem not,'' I said in answer to Thomas's question. ''There was no sign of her at all at the Crossed Hands when we reached there. She has simply disappeared. Gone to ground, perhaps, in case I accuse her of an attempt on my life; an attempt to which I have witnesses.''

''Indeed, yes,'' Thomas replied, laughing. ''Though witnesses who are not the most respectable of citizens.'' He refilled Master Parsons's cup before turning once more to me. "So what will you do now, lad? Will you be on your way in the morning, or will you remain a while longer and pursue your quest for what became of Clement Weaver?"

I hesitated, staring into the heart of the glowing fire. For the first time since I arrived in London, I felt unsure of my purpose. This evening's adventure had provided a climax to my first visit after which everything else seemed of little importance. In my mind I went back over the events of the past few hours.

As soon as I had finished telling the Duke my story, he had leapt to his feet, shouting for one of his squires to dress him. The children's nurse had been summoned to take them to bed, and a page sent scurrying into the ante-room to give orders for a posse of His Grace's men to accompany him to Crooked Lane. In the middle of this whirl of activity, the Duchess of York had sat unmoving, until, finally, she had risen and placed her hands on her youngest son's shoulders.

"Richard," she had said gravely, "if this story should prove to be true, promise me that you'll take no action against this Martin Trollope. If you do, George is bound to be implicated. Now that I have you all together again, I want nothing to come between him and Edward. The Queen's family hate George and will stop at nothing to harm him. Please don't give them any more reason than they have already."

The Duke had paused, looking deep into her eyes, then, with a sigh, he had leaned forward and kissed his mother on the forehead. "Very well. If I find Anne safe and well, I'll lay no charges." He had added with a wry smile: "I'm fond of George, too, damn him!"

And so, when we finally arrived at the Crossed Hands inn, after a ride in which I rode pillion behind my little friend rescued from the pieman, there had been no arrests, no violence, only a polite, but deadly quiet request to be conducted to the Lady Anne Neville. I had expected bluster and denials from Martin Trollope, but he must have seen from the Duke's eyes that the game was up, because my lord was conducted upstairs at once. No one was witness to his reunion with his cousin, or heard what they said to one another, but when the Duke finally brought her down to the courtyard, her eyes shone like stars. I don't think, either before or since, I have ever seen two people more in love than Richard of Gloucester and Lady Anne Neville.

After a few scathing words for Martin Trollope, and some words for me which I have already related, the Duke and his lady had departed for St. Martin-le-Grand, but some of his men had been left behind. It was the one condition I had daringly laid down, before telling His Grace my story, that the inn premises should be thoroughly searched, particularly the cellars. I had been hoping to discover evidence of murder and robbery, and I think the Duke had been hoping so, too, because then he could have brought charges against Martin Trollope on counts not involving his brother. But there was no evidence to find, and my accusations had brought strenuous denials from the landlord. He denied with equal vigor sending Matilda Ford after me this evening to kill me, and protested that he had been unaware either of my suspicions or my intentions. And, as I said, I found myself believing his story.

So where did that leave my quest for the truth concerning Clement Weaver? No doubt God still wished me to continue, but I was suddenly too tired to care. I felt I had done enough; and perhaps, after all, in finding the Lady Anne and restoring her to the man she loved I had fulfilled God's purpose. Maybe Clement Weaver and Sir Richard Mallory had been merely the means to an end, and I had mistaken God's real intention. Yes; that was it. I had achieved what I had been sent to London to do and now I could move on.

I had a sudden yearning for the countryside; for the forests and moorland, the scattered villages and hamlets, the walled towns islanded in seas of green. I wanted to hear the lapping of streams over pebbles, smell the acrid scent of distant bonfires, see the swirling morning mists. I had enjoyed London, but I had had enough of it. I was ready to move on.

"I shall be leaving in the morning," I said, raising my eyes from their contemplation of the flames and smiling at Thomas Prynne. "Thank you for your hospitality, but after tonight I shan't be troubling you again."

"No trouble, no trouble at all!" he exclaimed a shade too heartily, and I realized that he was probably relieved. He and Abel did too little business at the Baptist's Head to offer free lodgings for any length of time. It was only my acquaintance with Marjorie Dyer which had made him feel obliged to take me in . . . The name of Marjorie Dyer brought me up short as I remembered her connection with Matilda Ford and the Crossed Hands inn. I felt the stirrings of unease again, as though God were reminding me that I had not accomplished all my mission. There was something I still had not discovered about that place, I was sure of it.

"Anything wrong, lad?" Thomas Prynne inquired, evidently noting some change in my expression.

"No, no," I lied hurriedly, "nothing at all. And now, if you'll forgive me, I'll go to bed. I shall sleep like the dead tonight. I don't think I've ever been so tired."

Thomas nodded and got up to light my candle. "We shall see you in the morning, then, at breakfast, to say our farewells."

"Er—Yes. Yes. Good night, Master Parsons."

"We shan't meet again, then," he said, rising to his feet and holding out his hand.

"No . . . No, I don't suppose so."

I caught an exchange of glances between Thomas and Abel, and realized that my hesitations had revealed my wavering purpose. They had been hoping to get rid of me; now, they could sense that I was on the verge of changing my mind. Thomas sought to help me change it back again.

He clapped me on the shoulder. "As it's your last night with us, you shall have the very best room. A fitting end to an eventful sojourn in London. What do you say, Abel? As Master Farmer still hasn't turned up, let our chapman friend have his bed."

"By all means!" Abel agreed, giving me a friendly smile. "A man who has rendered service to the Duke of Gloucester deserves only the finest this inn can offer. Furthermore, Roger shall be treated like an honored guest. Half a loaf of white bread and a jug of our best wine for his all-night."

"Of course!" Thomas was beaming. "Why didn't I think of that? And one of us will lend you a night-shirt. Unless your pack includes such an item?"

I shook my head ruefully. "When would I use it?"

"True! True!" Abel said, laughing. "Bring your candle and let me conduct you to bed. For one night, at least, you can sleep like a prince. That mattress is the best in London."

I took this with the proverbial pinch of salt, as no doubt I was meant to, and followed Abel upstairs to the room I had noted early that morning. Abel set the candle down on top of the oak cupboard, beside the one already there in the pewter holder. The halo of light illuminated the huge four-poster bed with its tester and curtains of rubbed red velvet, and was reflected in the polished metal of the mirror. The clothes-chest was now shut and I could see that its heavy lid was intricately carved with a pattern of intertwined roses. The scent of lavender and spices, however, still lingered on the air.

As I set down my pack and stick, which I had brought up with me, Thomas came in carrying a tray bearing the promised all-night, and with a night-shirt draped over one arm. "Here we are, then, lad," he said, depositing the first on top of the cupboard and tossing the other on to the bed. "Sleep well. We'll see you in the morning."

I thanked them both, at the same time wondering how I was going to break it to them tomorrow that I had changed my mind and intended to stay a while longer in London. Perhaps I could find other lodgings, but the prospect daunted me. Besides, I wanted to be near the Crossed Hands inn. I started to undo the laces of my tunic, wondering what had become of Matilda Ford, but I was really too weary to care. I was paying the price for the excitement of the past few hours and the exertions of the day. My whole body ached and my mind felt clogged with dreams. I looked forward to undressing; to ridding myself of the clothes I had worn for so many days; to putting on the soft, white night-shirt and tumbling into bed; to consuming my all-night at leisure before finally closing my eyes.

But it was not to be. I allowed myself to drop back against the goose-feather pillows for a moment, my tunic still half unlaced, and I must straightway have fallen asleep. Almost at once, I was in the middle of a strange, wild dream. I was in Pudding Street, outside the whore-house, and the cloaked figure was advancing on me, knife upraised, but I could neither move or speak. Susan and the other prostitutes were there behind me, but they were laughing and jeering, doing nothing to help. I heard one of them say: "The man's a fool, a common chapman!" and another one answered: "What can you expect?" My assailant was nearly upon me now, and the hood fell back from the livid face. The foxy-colored hair and pale blue eyes were Matilda Ford's, but while I watched, petrified, she seemed to grow and the features became those of Abel Sampson. "We've been expecting you! Expecting you!" he whispered, his voice gradually fading away . . .

The scene changed abruptly, as happens in dreams. I was no longer outside Mother Bindloss's, but sitting with Robert, Lady Mallory's steward, in his room next to the buttery in Tuffnel Manor. "His passion was wine," Robert was saying, over and over again. "His passion was wine." And I knew that he was talking about Sir Richard Mallory. Once more, the scene dissolved, and I was lying with Bess by the banks of the Stour. I wanted to make love to her, but she wouldn't let me. "Where is he?" she kept asking. "Where's Master Farmer?"

Suddenly I was wide awake, sweating profusely in the darkness. For a moment or two my thoughts were in total confusion and I had difficulty in recalling exactly where I was. Then, as consciousness returned, everything fell simply and easily into place . . .

What a fool I had been! What a blind, stupid ass not to have seen what, all along, was under my nose. The disappearance of Clement Weaver, Sir Richard Mallory and his man, and doubtless a dozen or so others, had nothing to do with the Crossed Hands inn nor with Martin Trollope. It was here, in the Baptist's Head, that they had been robbed and murdered.

I pulled myself up into a sitting position, my back propped against the pillows. I was trembling with fear and excitement and, above all, the shock of discovery. Reaching for the half loaf of bread beside my bed, I tore a piece off and crammed it into my mouth. In moments of stress, I am always hungry. I glanced around me. The candle had gone out, and all the furniture of the room had assumed nocturnally gigantic proportions. It was late and everything was still. Once, an owl hooted, its desolate cry echoing weirdly over the roof-tops. Somewhere in the distance a horse snorted and stamped, one man called to another, a dog barked. Then silence drifted back, more profound than before. Wisps of smoke from the candle still hung about the room, uneasy spirits in search of a home.

I shivered violently. My mouth was dry and I had a job to swallow the bread. My hand went out for the jug of wine and the cup, then remained suspended in midair, hovering over the tray. I remembered the deep sleep into which I had fallen the previous evening, and realized for the first time that I might not have been drunk, but drugged. I recalled how disconcerted Thomas Prynne had been to find me up and awake in the middle of the night. He had not counted on the strength of my general constitution.

I withdrew my hand and sat up even straighter on the bed, trying to arrange my thoughts in order.

CHAPTER
19

First and foremost, there had only been Thomas Prynne's word that Clement Weaver had never arrived at the Baptist's Head. And because Clement had last been seen outside the Crossed Hands inn, everyone, including myself, had allowed themselves to believe that his disappearance might have something to do with the latter. Whereas the truth was that he must have walked down to the Baptist's Head to be greeted with affection by the murderous pair. He trusted them. Thomas was his father's friend; the boyhood friend, who had grown up to be deeply envious of the other man's success. So envious, that he had moved from Bristol to London in an attempt to make his own fortune.

Thomas had bought the Baptist's Head; but its location and the fact that it was overshadowed by the rival inn further up the lane had meant only very small profit for a lot of hard work. I had no means of knowing when and how he had met up with Abel Sampson, but I guessed that like had called to like. They were both ambitious, greedy and unscrupulous men. Together they had devised a scheme to murder and rob their wealthiest clients. Not all of them, of course, that would have been impossible; just those traveling alone or with a single servant. Maybe they had informants in various parts of the country, like Marjorie Dyer in Bristol, whose job it was to recommend the Baptist's Head to any such people. She must have forewarned Thomas that, on this particular occasion, Clement Weaver was carrying an unusually large sum of money.

But Marjorie sent her letters to Matilda Ford at the Crossed Hands inn. That, of course, was a precaution in case anyone ever became suspicious. Matilda Ford certainly worked at the rival inn, but the first time I had seen her, she had reminded me of someone. And that someone was Abel Sampson. I wondered how I could have been so blind as not to see it. Hadn't I said to myself that she was nothing like Marjorie Dyer? And I had only just left Abel at the Baptist's Head. The resemblance—the sandy hair, the height, the thinness—had been staring me in the face, yet I had been unable to recognize it. I had no means of knowing what their relationship actually was, but guessed it was probably that of brother and sister. Perhaps Abel himself had once worked at the Crossed Hands inn and that was how Thomas had met him.

I went over once again in my mind the circumstances of Clement Weaver's disappearance. His arrival alone and on foot must have seemed like a gift from heaven to Thomas and Abel: they had only Clement to get rid of. The disposal of their victims' horses must always have presented a problem, but no doubt there were many shady dealers in London, and the sale of the animals had added more money to their coffers.

In the case of Sir Richard Mallory and his servant, Jacob Pender, the horses had remained at the Crossed Hands, to be claimed and taken away later by Sir Gregory Bullivant. I could not know for certain, but I had no doubt now in my mind that Sir Richard had been lured to the Baptist's Head after a "chance" meeting with either Thomas or Abel, during which he had been promised the finest wine he had ever tasted. Matilda would have informed the two men of Sir Richard's presence, told them that he was a bird worth the plucking, and that, in Robert the steward's words to me, he would "travel miles, brave all hazards, to taste a recommended vintage." The maid at the Crossed Hands had told Sir Gregory Bullivant that she had seen Sir Richard and his servant apparently arguing in the inn courtyard. At that point their saddle-bags had been packed and they were ready to leave, so it was likely that Jacob Pender had been protesting against delay, but his master had overruled him. They had walked the short distance to the Baptist's Head—and to their deaths . . .

Suddenly I could no longer endure the darkness and, leaning over, I fumbled for the tinder-box on the table beside me. The palms of my hands were sweating so much that I had great difficulty in coaxing a spark from it, but eventually I managed to light one of the candles. The flickering light cast distorted shadows which sent grotesque patterns leaping across the walls and ceiling. In my mind's eye I could see the two unsuspecting men being led down the ale-room steps and into the cellar.

I lay back on the pillows, shivering. I remembered seeing Abel Sampson for the first time yesterday morning and thinking he was like Richard of Gloucester when he smiled. But then, to repeat myself, in those days I was a poor judge of character. I remembered, too, his words on seeing me. "Is this the man we've been expecting?" And Thomas's reply: "No, no! I'm sure I told you that Master Farmer would not be arriving until late this evening." I recalled now the emphasis he had laid on the name and realized its significance. Months ago, Marjorie Dyer must have warned them of my involvement in Alfred Weaver's affairs; to be on the lookout for a chapman who might start asking awkward questions. I was indeed the man Abel had been expecting; although they must both have thought by then that I had changed my mind, or forgotten my commission, and was not coming.

Another memory stirred; something which at the time had troubled me, but which had been pushed to the back of my mind and its significance lost. Abel had immediately addressed me as Roger. I had told Thomas my name when I had told him my story, but there was no way his partner could have know, unless he had already been informed of it by Marjorie Dyer. But what of Matilda Ford's attack on me this afternoon? If Martin Trollope had not sent her, then who had? The answer, of course, was obvious now that I knew. Either Abel or Thomas had hurried to the Crossed Hands inn as soon as I had left for Baynard's Castle, routed her out from the kitchen and told her to follow and dispose of me if she could. But why? Answer: because although they had no particular wish to protect Martin Trollope, they did not want Richard of Gloucester's attention drawn to Crooked Lane and the tale of mysterious disappearances poured into his ear. And where was Matilda Ford now? Probably lurking somewhere on the premises. She dared not return to the Crossed Hands in case I had laid information against her.

My blood ran cold at the thought. I sat petrified, an animal scenting danger and too terrified to move. I pictured her creeping up the stairs, one of Thomas's wicked-looking kitchen knives poised and ready . . . What a crass fool I was! If I had not let Abel and Thomas see so plainly that I had changed my mind about moving on tomorrow morning, I should most likely have escaped unharmed.

Without having any recollection of moving, I found myself on my feet, trying to lace up my tunic with unsteady fingers. I must go now, at once, while Master Parsons—whose pockets were so to let that he was not worth killing—was still up and about. I must make any excuse and leave. Perhaps if I went to St. Paul's I could find Philip Lamprey and a makeshift bed in the cloisters. I had my cloak around me, my pack and stick in one hand, the other on the door latch, when I knew with a flash of blinding certainty that I could not do it. I could not leave Thomas Prynne and Abel Sampson to their murderous pursuits; I could not let other unsuspecting flies walk into their evil web. I had to find proof of what they were up to. And when better than now? The night after Master Farmer had, according to them, failed to arrive.

And I knew then, with complete certainty, that of course he had arrived while I, and no doubt Master Parsons, too, lay upstairs in a drugged sleep. He had been killed and his body disposed of sometime during the small hours before Matins and Lauds, when force of habit had dragged me awake. But surely they could not have rid themselves of everything so soon. Some trace of the unfortunate man must remain somewhere. But where? And there again, I did not have to seek far for an answer. The cellar was the only safe place for the murders; and undoubtedly the opening to the conduit, spoken of by the ragwoman, Doll, could be found there. It made far more sense than looking for it at the Crossed Hands inn: the Baptist's Head was so much closer to the wharfside and river.

Another question posed itself. If my theory were right and Master Farmer had arrived, what had happened to his horse? Then I remembered. I was sure I had heard two horses while I was in the privy last night. Later, Thomas Prynne had convinced me that I had heard only one, and at the time I had had no reason to disbelieve him. It explained, too, why the back door to the inn had been unbolted. Matilda Ford had been let in that way and it had been left unlocked until after her departure. Abel, too, had possibly been out of doors, in which case I had locked him out. The thought gave me a grim satisfaction.

My elation, however, was brief and immediately replaced by a sinking feeling in the pit of my stomach. What was I doing, contemplating, even for a moment, staying on at the Baptist's Head? I was deliberately putting myself in untold danger. For I had no doubt that the wine was drugged, nor that Thomas and Abel intended to dispose of me while I slept. I had become too much of a threat to their peace of mind. Only my immediate departure could save me now.

Besides, putting my own life in jeopardy had never been part of my bargain with God, and I told him so in no uncertain terms. Unfortunately, He did not seem to be listening.

"I won't do it," I muttered fiercely. "You have no right to ask it of me. You're omnipotent. You find a way of dealing with Thomas and Abel."

God remained silent, but I could tell that He wasn't pleased. Words like "coward" and "lily-livered" floated in and out of my mind. I thought of Alfred Weaver and Lady Mallory and my promises to them to find out the truth. Well, I had found out the truth, but unless I did something about it, I could never tell them. My knees were shaking, my mouth was dry and I gripped my pack and stick more firmly. My hand tightened on the latch . . . But I couldn't lift it. Bitterly I recognized the fact that, as always, God was going to get His own way.

I replaced pack and stick on the floor and took off my cloak, forcing my reluctant body to lie down on the bed again. There was an hour or two yet before everyone retired to bed and the inn was quiet. Until then, I could not carry out my purpose. I blew out the candle and lay there in the darkness, wondering how I was going to while away the time. I supposed I could always pray . . .

Against all expectations, I slept.

I awoke from a deep, dreamless sleep, the sweat pouring down my body. How could I possibly have dozed off when I knew my life to be in danger? I had heard stories of condemned men sleeping soundly the night before their execution, but had never believed them. Now I knew that exhaustion of body can sometimes overcome even fear.

I sat up, straining my ears. I had no idea how long I had been asleep, but the inn was very quiet. I slid off the bed, went over to the door and opened it a crack. All was silent, except for the noise of a stertorous, rhythmic snoring. I judged this to be coming from Master Parson's room, and knew with a sudden, horrible certainty that his supper wine had been drugged. Nothing would rouse him to come to my assistance. Moreover, he was expecting me to leave in the morning. Abel and Thomas would simply tell him that I had gone earlier than expected.

Softly I closed the door and leaned against the wall, trying to stop my teeth chattering. I reminded God tersely that He had got me into this mess and that it was up to Him to get me out of it. He reminded me that he had given me strength, health and a thinking brain and that it was up to me to use these precious assets. I abandoned the argument. Why could I never learn that it was useless trying to burden God with my responsibilities?

After a moment or two, when I was more in control of my body, I began to edge towards the door again. I must get out of the room before Abel or Thomas or Matilda Ford came to complete their handiwork. I didn't think they would hurry. They thought me drugged, and would wait until they were certain that Master Parsons was soundly sleeping. I had one advantage: neither Thomas nor Abel were aware that I knew the truth. They still thought that my suspicions were centered on the Crossed Hands inn. I stooped and picked up the stout, thick stick which had supported me across so many miles. Now, I needed it for a different purpose. As silently as possible, I again lifted the latch.

The landing was in darkness except for the light which filtered through the window shutters. Cautiously I stepped across and opened them a fraction, peering down into the street. Tonight, however, there was no sign of life; no cloaked and hooded figure making her way along Crooked Lane. Closing the shutters once more, I returned to the head of the stairs and listened intently for any sound of voices from below. I could hear nothing and proceeded to tiptoe downstairs in my stockinged feet, stepping carefully so as to avoid any tell-tale creaking. Each moment I expected to be challenged by one or the other of the villainous trio.

At the bottom of the flight I waited, my back pressed against the wall, my ears straining for the slightest sound, my cudgel gripped securely in my right hand, ready for instant action. Still there was only silence and a complete absence of light. Had Thomas and Abel gone upstairs to bed, keeping vigil in their respective chambers until such time as they were sure the drugged wine had taken effect? Or were they still down here, ready to waylay me in the darkness? My heart was pounding so fast, I felt as if I must choke. I took a deep breath, trying to stop its frantic beating.

"Put yourself in their place," said a voice inside my head, and I obeyed it. Why should they wait downstairs for me, when they had no idea that I was likely to leave my room? When they believed me safely tucked up in the four-poster, fast asleep, drugged by the wine? I must force myself to remember that they had no reason to know that I had tumbled to their murderous little game. If they were still up, they would be working in the kitchen, preparing the bread for tomorrow's early morning baking. But there was no light and no noise from that quarter.

I wondered what o'clock it was, and cursed myself for having fallen asleep. If they had come for me then . . . ! My blood ran cold at the thought. But they had had to wait for Master Parsons to retire, to drink his drugged wine and for the wine to take effect. And now it had. Surely they could hear that as well as I. It could not be long now before they went to my room and discovered I was not there. I must be swift if I wanted to search the cellar. I was wasting precious minutes while I stood here imagining Thomas and Abel lying in ambush for me. I had proved to myself that there was no reason why they should be. Stealthily I crept into the ale-room.

All was quiet here, too. My eyes were now completely accustomed to the darkness, and I made my way between the benches and tables without difficulty. I knelt on the floor by the far wall and felt around, among the sand and sawdust, for the heavy metal ring which, when pulled, opened the trapdoor to the cellar. I found it easily, and, laying my stick down, got to my feet, stooped, clasped the ring in both hands and began to tug. Sweat, however, had made my hands slippery and for several moments I could get no purchase on it. Cursing silently, I wiped my greasy palms against my tunic, then tried again. This time the stone slab rose almost too swiftly and I had to let go the ring to catch it against my body, in order to prevent it thudding on to the floor. When I had lowered it gently to the ground, I peered down the flight of steps leading to the cellar.

At once I realized that I should need a light, and again called myself all the names I could lay my tongue to for not having foreseen such a contingency. I should have brought one of the candles from the bedchamber with me. Now, I would have to go and find one in the kitchen. Every moment wasted made my discovery more likely, but there was nothing I could do about it. I should find nothing in the cellar in pitch blackness.

I made my way back to the passageway, my ears pricked for the sound of any movement above stairs; but still all I could hear was the noise of Master Parsons's snoring. It was probably not as late as I thought, and my sleep had been briefer than I imagined. The small hours, the dead time of night, were best for murder . . . I shuddered and cast a longing look at the inn's front door, clearly silhouetted at one end of the passage. I could go now; make my escape while I had the opportunity. I even took a step towards the door before conscience halted me in my tracks. If I went, I could prove nothing. There were only my suspicions against Thomas and Abel's denials; and I had no doubt that within hours of discovering I had gone, the inn would be swept clean of the last trace of anything damning. And although my allegations might make the authorities keep their eye on the Baptist's Head for a while, they would soon tire when nothing further happened. And Thomas and Abel would make sure of that for as long as was necessary.

Reluctantly I turned in the opposite direction, towards the kitchen, and at first I thought it was still in darkness. But as I approached the open door, I could see a faint glow. Hardly daring to breathe, I flattened myself against the wall, my hand tightening unconsciously around my cudgel. After a moment or two I could hear slight movements. As cautiously as I dared, I peered round the jamb of the doorway. The source of the illumination was a rush-light, which explained its dim uncertainty, but it was sufficient for me to make out a woman sitting at the table, eating.

Once more, I leaned against the wall, trying to quieten my thumping heart. The woman could only be Matilda Ford, and my fears that she had taken refuge in the inn had been only too well-founded.

She must have been somewhere around when I crept downstairs, but fortunately she had not seen me. If she had been aware of my presence, she would surely not be sat in the kitchen, fortifying herself for the night's work which lay ahead of her . . . Not for the first, nor the last, time since supper, I found that I was shaking.

There was no chance now of obtaining a candle from the kitchen. And there was no possible use in braving the cellar in total darkness. It was, I told myself, clearly a sign that I should leave. God had changed His mind and no longer wished me to risk my skin. I was freed from my promise to Alderman Weaver. I began tiptoeing along the passage towards the front door. I was nearly there. Another few steps and I should be able to draw the bolts and let myself out into Crooked Lane and freedom.

A hand fell heavily on my shoulder and, as I spun round, a light shone full in my eyes.

"Leaving us, Roger Chapman?" asked Thomas's voice, and I could just make out his face, framed in the aureole of the candle. Abel was standing in the middle of the stairs, behind him. Matilda Ford appeared in the kitchen doorway, a slice of bread still held in one hand.

Stupidly I stared back at them, the thought uppermost in my mind being that I should have known better than to think that God would let me go back on my promise.

CHAPTER
20

The smoke from the candle made my eyes water, and the flame bellied into pale, wavering circles with scalloped, iridescent edges. I just stood there stupidly, a great dumb ox, saying nothing. But what, after all, was there to say? I could hardly claim to be going for a midnight walk.

Thomas said, smiling a little: "I wondered if the truth might dawn on you, but I was hoping for your sake it wouldn't; that you'd drink the wine and go to sleep, so you'd never know what had happened to you." He added regretfully: "I've grown fond of you, Roger, in the short time that we've been acquainted." Abel muttered something I couldn't quite catch, but Thomas heard, and his smile deepened. He did not, however, make the mistake of turning his head. "Oh, I know you don't care for our young guest, Abel, but when you're my age, you'll begin to appreciate loyalty. He gave his word to poor old Alfred Weaver, and nothing would persuade him to change his mind. I admire that."

I found my tongue. "You lying, murdering, robbing hypocrite!" I shouted at him, raising my stick and dashing the candle from his hand.

Thomas swore furiously as the flame burnt his leg in its fall and extinguished itself on the flagstones. Then all three were upon me, trying to grapple me to the floor. In the end, they succeeded, being three to one, but not before I had done considerable damage with my cudgel. By the time they had manhandled me into the ale-room and Thomas had produced a tinder-box from his pocket to relight the candle, Abel was bleeding copiously from his nose and had a fast-swelling eye, Matilda had an evil-looking weal across one cheek and Thomas himself was limping painfully. All three regarded me with venomous hatred.

"You know," Abel grunted softly, wiping the blood from his face with the back of his hand, "I shall positively enjoy this night's work."

Matilda had produced a coil of tough hempen rope from somewhere and they proceeded to bind my arms and legs. I struggled wildly, although I knew I was beaten before they began. Then Thomas took my head and Abel my feet and carried me, like a fowl trussed ready for the oven, towards the cellar steps. Matilda went ahead of them, holding up the candle. All was suddenly very quiet. Even Gilbert Parsons had stopped snoring. I opened my mouth and yelled.

Thomas chuckled grimly. "Shout all you want," he said, "no one will hear you. Master Parsons is dead to the world. And very few people come this way after curfew."

I knew he was right. And if, by some remote chance, anyone did hear my call for help, they were unlikely to venture into the inn on my behalf. Londoners minded their own business after dark, and were undoubtedly wise to do so.

As I was bundled down the cellar steps, my head knocked against the wall and I was partially stunned for a moment or two. By the time I fully recovered my senses, I had been dropped on the floor and Thomas was lighting a second candle. I saw the cellar was much bigger than I had expected, and, by my calculations, ran not only beneath the house itself, but also almost to the edge of the wharf which skirted it on one side. The walls were lined with wine-racks supporting a great many bottles, and the stone floor was covered patchily with straw. Noises came to my ears; a slight scuffling sound which I knew must be rats, and the faint lapping of water, which confirmed my guess that we must be very close to the Thames.

I turned my head to observe my captors. Abel had picked up a thick crowbar, and my blood ran cold. Then I noticed that Thomas had one also, and my heart almost stopped. They were going to club me to death! But they went over to the cellar wall which, by my reckoning, was nearest to the river, inserted the bars on either side of one of the massive stone slabs of which the walls were built, and levered it from its position. When it finally stood sufficiently proud, they laid down the bars and, straining and sweating, lifted it clear, depositing it finally on the floor. A dark, gaping hole was left in the wall, easily large enough to take a man's body, and I had no doubt that this was the way they disposed of their hapless victims. There must be an underground chute leading straight down into the water; the drain or conduit which had given Crooked Lane its original name.

In spite of my bonds, I managed to wriggle into a sitting position, but immediately Matilda Ford was behind me, her strong hands pressing me down.

"Leave him, Matty!" Thomas Prynne said, turning his head to see what was happening. "No reason why he shouldn't watch." He laughed. "He isn't going to tell anyone. Right, lad!" His eyes swiveled until they were focused directly on my face. "You'd better start saying your prayers."

"Wait!" I said, playing for time. God alone knew what good I thought it would do me, but the will to survive is man's strongest instinct, and I was no exception. I wanted to postpone the moment of my inevitable death as long as I possibly could. In answer to Thomas's look of inquiry, I went on: "If you're going to kill me, at least satisfy my curiosity first. It can't harm you now to tell me the truth."

"Don't listen to him," Matilda begged sharply, speaking for the first time since she had appeared on the scene, upstairs in the passageway. "Get rid of him quickly."

Abel nodded, his pale eyes gleaming. "Matty's right. Let's get on with it."

But Thomas was in the mood to humor me. I realized suddenly that he was a vain man, who was normally balked of talking about himself and his murderous achievements.

"I see no reason why we shouldn't satisfy his curiosity if he wishes. In any case, it shouldn't take long. I imagine he knows most of what we can tell him already. You're a bright young man," he added, addressing me directly. "When and why did you finally tumble to the truth?"

"When I went up to bed this evening. As to why, let's just say that Abel made one or two slips that ought to have put me on your track much earlier, if I hadn't been so dull-witted. And Mistress Ford here reminded me of someone the first time I met her. Again, it wasn't until tonight that I realized she looks like Abel."

Thomas smiled. "Observant of you. They're brother and sister. But I can see by your face that you'd already worked that out. Abel also used to be an ostler at the Crossed Hands inn. That's how we met, when I came to buy this place. I lured him away from Martin Trollope to work for me, and he proved to be worth his weight in gold. He knew the stories about the old smugglers' conduit running down to the wharfside, and eventually, after a lot of searching, we found it. To begin with, we considered using it for its original purpose, but smuggling puts you at the mercy of too many other people. We found a better use for it. I'm not sure now whose idea it was. I rather fancy it might have been Matilda's." He hesitated, loath to deny himself credit. "No, on second thoughts, I believe it was mine. We would run the inn to the very best of our ability, gaining a reputation for excellent wine and food. That way, sooner or later, we were bound to attract richer visitors to the inn."

"Whom you then cold-bloodedly murdered."

"Oh, not all of them." Thomas looked pained.

"Credit us with a little common sense, lad. The circumstances have to be exactly right. A solitary traveller, or with just one servant. And, of course, carrying a large sum of money or jewels about his person. Which is why it's a slow, waiting game, needing patience. And why we cannot risk being discovered. It will need many more years yet before the three of us are wealthy enough to retire."

"And in the meantime you all enjoy your work!" I flung at him.

Thomas considered this, a smile hovering about his lips. "I suppose that's true," he admitted, almost dreamily.

I felt my skin crawl. I also felt the impatience of the other two, and plunged on desperately. "And Mistress Ford informed you of any birds ripe for the plucking staying at the Crossed Hands inn?"

"Occasionally. You're thinking of Sir Richard Mallory. He was extremely easy. He loved fine wines, and all Matty had to do was to tell him that we had some of the best in London. She had no difficulty persuading him to come over and sample the contents of our cellar. Of course, we had to make sure that he brought his man with him, as well."

"Of course. You couldn't risk Jacob Pender being left behind to tell where his master had gone. And to wait until the last morning of Sir Richard's visit, when he had paid his reckoning and his saddle-bags were packed, that was a stroke of genius."

Thomas smiled benignly. "Naturally. The whole operation is always carefully planned."

"And Marjorie Dyer? How did you persuade her to join you?"

Thomas shrugged. "Nothing simpler. Marjorie has always been ambitious. She had hopes at one time of marrying Alfred Weaver. She may even have been instrumental in helping Mistress Weaver to her death, although I have no proof of that, you understand. Not that it matters. You won't be telling anyone of my suspicions. But Alfred foolishly failed to make her his wife, even though he continued to avail himself of her—er—services. Last year, while on a visit to Bristol, I took her into my confidence and found her willing enough to play my game. At a price, needless to say. Since when, she has directed at least two well-plumaged birds into our net, apart from Clement Weaver." He added regretfully: "Believe it or not, I was sorry to have to kill Clement. I've known him since childhood, you see."

"For God's sake, let's get on!" Abel hissed. "Do you mean to stand around here all night, talking?"

"Steady! Steady!" Thomas reproved him. "You're losing your nerve, and that will never do. However, you may be right." He looked at me. "Say your prayers, then, Roger Chapman. You've caused us a great deal of trouble, losing Matilda her place at the Crossed Hands and making her a hunted criminal. We really didn't want you running off to the Duke of Gloucester like that, and hoped to prevent you. But in spite of everything, we should still have let you go tomorrow morning as you planned, if you hadn't so obviously changed your mind in the middle of supper. A shame, but we really couldn't have you making yet more trouble. Besides, I calculated it wouldn't be long before you realized the truth. So!" He shrugged again. "There's nothing for it, I'm afraid, but to send you down the chute to join our other guests in their watery graves. Don't worry. You won't know anything about it, that's a promise."

"Why not?" Matilda demanded viciously. "Why knock him over the head? Let him know what's happening to him."

"Because we don't want him bound," her brother answered tersely. "In case his body's ever found, it must seem as though he simply fell into the river."

Matilda muttered something under her breath, then added aloud: "Then let me do it! I owe him a beating."

"A pleasure," Thomas said, and handed her my stick, which had been brought down to the cellar with me. "Use this. And not too hard, mind. We only want him unconscious."

"No!" I shouted. At least, I think that's what I shouted. To this day I can't recall exactly what I said. My brain had ceased to function, and all I remember is a burning rage against God, who, I felt, was responsible for my predicament. I began wriggling around violently on the floor, so that Matilda Ford's first swipe with my cudgel missed me by inches.

"Hold him still!" Thomas commanded Abel. "Sit on his legs!"

Abel threw himself to his knees and grabbed both my feet, pinning them to the ground. I kicked with all my might and loosened his grip, but only for a matter of seconds. He was on me again, this time pinioning me by the legs, while Thomas himself moved forward to assist. Their combined weight held me prisoner.

"Now, Matty!" her brother shouted.

She was at the back of me and it was impossible to twist my neck that far round. I wanted to meet death face to face, not be struck down from behind like some animal. I felt the rush of air as she raised her arm, and once again I shouted my defiance, trying to swing the upper half of my body out of the way. Thomas yelled something at his partner and their combined grip tightened. I knew that there was no real hope. I shut my eyes and waited for the blow to fall . . .

Nothing happened, while the moment of anticipation seemed to stretch on and on. After what seemed an agonizing eternity, I cautiously reopened my eyes, to see my captors staring, horror-struck and open-mouthed, in the direction of the cellar stairs. I realized that the two men were no longer sitting on my legs and I was free to move. I shuffled round as best I could until I, too, could see the flight of stone steps leading down from the ale-room. There were men standing there, quite a few of them, and the leader was holding up a lantern.

A voice said: "In the name of King Edward, I arrest you, Thomas Prynne, you, Abel Sampson, and you, Matilda Ford, on a charge of murder." The owner of the voice turned to the men behind him. "Take them away." Then the man himself jumped sideways off the flight of stairs and came towards me, holding his lantern higher so that it illuminated his face. "Well, Master Chapman," he said, smiling, "that was a close call. I was afraid I was going to be too late."

I had recognized the voice as soon as he spoke, but had refused to believe the evidence of my own ears. Gone was the gentle, slightly apologetic tone. Master Parsons now spoke with all the authority of one who had the might and weight of the Law behind him.

"I'm a Sheriff's officer," he explained later, as we sat together in the inn parlor, a bottle of Thomas Prynne's best wine on the table between us. It was quiet now, after the events of the past hour. Thomas and his two confederates had been bound and led away to prison, but I was still very shaken. Master Parsons poured more wine for us both and went on: "We've had suspicions about this place for some time now. Rumors have come to our ears of people who lodged here disappearing. But nothing we could prove, even to our own satisfaction. So it was finally decided that I should come to stay as a guest in the hope of discovering something."

"And did you?" I asked him.

He shook his head. "Not until you came along, poking your nose in."

"What about Master Farmer, last night?"

Gilbert Parsons shrugged. "He genuinely did not arrive. Oh, Thomas and Abel, together with Matilda Ford, were waiting like carrion crows to do their evil business, but on this occasion they were balked of their prey."

I protested: "I heard a second horse in the stables, when I went to the privy."

"Your imagination, I'm afraid." Master Parsons stretched his arms above his head until the bones cracked. "Jesu! I shall be glad to get out of this place and home for some sleep at nights. I've had precious little this past week."

I barely heard him. I was too busy wrestling with

my indignation. If I hadn't been convinced that I should find some trace of Master Farmer, I should never have risked looking in Thomas's cellar. God had fooled me again. All the same, I supposed I shouldn't complain. He had watched over me and seen that I came to no lasting harm. He had used me as his instrument, and my debt for leaving the abbey was now, I hoped, paid.

I smiled at my companion. "For a man who, according to himself, hasn't slept at nights, you snore very loudly."

Gilbert laughed. "A trick I learned as a child to deceive my mother. My brothers and I used to take it in turns to do the snoring while the others played five-stones or spillikins under the sheets." He finished the wine in his cup and stretched again. "It's almost daylight. Do you feel strong enough to come with me and swear you deposition before a magistrate?"

"I think so." I, too, finished my wine, fighting down the urge to curl up in a corner and fall asleep. My first two days in London were days I would never forget, not even if I lived to be a very old man. For now, I should be glad to put the city behind me and get out once more on the open road, but one day I would return. I recollected that I had visits to pay to Canterbury and Bristol; particularly to the latter.

It would give me great pleasure to make sure that Marjorie Dyer's part in this villainy was known. I glanced towards the cellar steps, where the trapdoor still lay open, revealing the cavernous hole in the floor.

"How did you know what was happening?" I asked.

"I heard you yell." Gilbert Parsons grinned. "I guessed, when you made it so plain that you had changed your mind about moving on this morning, that they might try to silence you, but not that you would do anything as foolish as to try searching the inn on your own. I crept downstairs just in time to see them carrying you off, trussed up like a chicken to the cellar, and went immediately for help. I must admit that I despaired of rescuing you in time."

"Well," I said feelingly, "I'm very thankful you did." I reached for my pack and stick, which I had brought down from the bedchamber earlier and which now lay beside my chair. "I'm ready to go if you are. I don't want to see this evil place again as long as I live."

Gilbert Parsons nodded and we went out into Crooked Lane, breathing in the cold morning air. A seagull screeched overhead, looking for food. The Baptist's Head lay behind us, shuttered and silent. At the top of the street, the Crossed Hands still teemed with life. Lady Anne Neville was safely in sanctuary; Martin Trollope, protected by the Duke of Clarence, still walked free. Thomas Prynne, Abel Sampson and Matilda Ford were locked up in prison and would pay for their crimes with their lives. But Clement Weaver, Sir Richard Mallory and others would never return, and I felt inexpressibly sad.

And that, my children—if you have bothered to read this far—is how it all started, that talent I discovered in myself, and honed over the years, of solving puzzles and unraveling mysteries. Of course, this first case was full of flaws and mistakes and stupid bungling because I was raw and green and still wet behind the ears. I didn't really know what I was doing or letting myself in for. It happened partly because of my natural inquisitiveness, and partly because of that stubborn streak in my nature which hates to let anything go without seeing it through to the end.

Oh yes; and God had a hand in it somewhere. He always does. He's as stubborn and as tenacious as I am about getting His own way. I've tried to free myself from Him often and often, but somehow I never could. And now that I'm an old man living on memories, I think I'm glad that I haven't succeeded.

KATE SEDLEY has created a most unusual and charming sleuth in Roger the Chapman, who makes his debut in *Death and the Chapman*. A student of Anglo-Saxon and medieval history, Sedley lives in England.